"Just stay away from my son!"

Hands closed on her shoulders from behind. "Don't talk with him and don't play chess with him," Coffee continued as she shrugged her shoulders at his touch. But Dodge didn't let go. If anything, his grip tightened. She closed her eyes, trying not to shiver as she felt each individual fingertip press into her flesh.

"How long are you staying here?" She put an edge to that question.

His laugh was rueful, seductive, his breath warm on her ear. "Long as it takes to write your husband's biography. So if you want me out of town that badly . . ."

"Yes?"

"You ought to cooperate," he said softly, and let her go.

Peggy Nicholson, daughter of a Texas
wildcatter, comes by her risk taking naturally.
Despite a fear of heights, she has dabbled in rock
climbing and has been known to climb scaffolding
to repaint her Rhode Island home when needed.
She's been a teacher, an artist and a restorer of
antique yachts. But her two main passions are
sailing and writing, which, she insists, are all the
better when combined. As Peggy says, ''I can't
imagine a nicer way to live.''

Books by Peggy Nicholson

HARLEQUIN ROMANCE
3009—TENDER OFFER
3100—BURNING DREAMS

HARLEQUIN PRESENTS
732—THE DARLING JADE
741—RUN SO FAR
764—DOLPHINS FOR LUCK

HARLEQUIN SUPERROMANCE
193—SOFT LIES, SUMMER LIGHT
237—CHILD'S PLAY
290—THE LIGHT FANTASTIC

CHECKMATE
Peggy Nicholson

Harlequin Books

TORONTO • NEW YORK • LONDON
AMSTERDAM • PARIS • SYDNEY • HAMBURG
STOCKHOLM • ATHENS • TOKYO • MILAN

ISBN 0-373-03172-6

Harlequin Romance first edition January 1992

CHECKMATE

CHAPTER ONE

WHY WON'T THEY leave us alone? Oh, why won't they leave us alone? It didn't make a good marching rhyme. The question was too complex, too many syllables.

Point and counterpoint, the tips of Coffee Dugan's ski poles jabbed into the heavy snow. Her cross-country skis attacked the hill with a two-note ripping sound. *Leave us. Leave us.* That's what her skis and the snow and her heart were crying. As she raced up the trail, her breath steamed out, billowing around her flushed cheeks, then pluming above her mane of golden, flyaway hair.

Her round chin lifted at a flicker of yellow beyond the trees above her, where the trail steepened and bent out of sight. She stepped out of the groomed track into the deeper snow to the side of the path and stood there, panting. Trail etiquette decreed that downhill skiers always took right-of-way. And in the town of Jackson, New Hampshire, the descending skier was apt to be a tourist, and a novice on the slopes—white knuckled and on the ragged edge of control. Right-of-way or no, the prudent native stepped aside. Foreign entanglements could take on a whole new meaning when two strangers met on skis.

But this skier was rounding the last bend above her with the deceptive smoothness of an expert. He saw her, smiled as he passed, then his edges bit into the snow. He snowplowed to a stop just below her, his skis a precise V, and looked back over his shoulder. "Coffee."

"Hello, Peter." She stepped back into the track. Much as she liked the ski patrolman, this was no day for chatting. She had to get home to her son, get him out of town. She'd take Jeffie to a movie down in North Conway, stay for supper and maybe some shopping. By the time they came home, whoever had been looking for them would be—

"Coffee, wait. I was trying to find you. Somebody's been asking around town about—"

"I heard. Lisa told me down at the store." A stranger, Lisa had said, in a sleek black sports car, asking for the family of Richard Dugan. No one had come asking for nearly a year now. *Oh, why won't they leave us alone?*

"He stopped by Hilltop Farm. Asked Ike if somebody ⸺d Maureen owned the place."

Coffee ⸺ ⸺s widened. "Maureen!" So the stranger knew the name o. ⸺ichard Dugan's mother, Coffee's mother-in-law. That wa. a first. Usually the reporters simply came looking for the Dugan family.

And the town collectively and singly turned them away with a shrug, with a smiling shake of the head, with a Yankee's laconic, "Wouldn't know." Because if Maureen and Coffee Dugan didn't want to talk to reporters, that was that, as far as anyone who knew anything in Jackson was concerned.

Peter turned to stand parallel to her. "Ike didn't tell him anything, of course."

Of course. But the stranger had known somehow that Maureen owned a bed and breakfast, even if he'd chosen the wrong one. And there weren't that many in town to choose from. If he went asking at each and every one... "I've got to get home, Peter!"

"I just came from there. Nobody's home but Jeffie and one of your guests. They're playing a game out in the sunroom."

view, Coffee stood paralyzed, willing this not to be so. It *had* to be a dream.

In her mind's eye, she saw not the varnished oak beneath her fingertips, but a chessboard, in close-up on the television screen, with her husband's long fingers descending into camera range, the chessman he held coming down like a falling axe. She took a sobbing breath as the camera in her memory switched to Richard Dugan's opponent, mercilessly probing his reaction. The look on the Russian's face had been fear—a fear so deep, so physical, that her own stomach had twisted with pity and revulsion. They called this a game? No one should be made to feel such fear! So she had switched the TV off, had watched no more of the tournament in which Richard had won the world championship without losing a single match.

"If you move it there, Jeff, what will my queen do?" The voice was low, male, and unfamiliar to Coffee, and its question confirmed her worse fears. Taking a deep, shaking breath, she stepped into the room.

Jeffie and the stranger were playing in front of the fire. The chessboard that sat on the rug between them was tiny, some sort of traveling, folding set similar to the one Richard had carried with him wherever he went. Across the board, man and child faced each other. Their poses mirrored each other exactly—legs crossed Indian fashion, hands on knees, her son's white-blond head and the stranger's dark one bent over to study the game. But if their positions were identical, their attitudes were not. The stranger sat with the lithe, loose-jointed ease of a big cat. Jeffie sat with a furious, forward-leaning immobility, as if he were about to dive into the game. His attention was directed at the board like a blaze of light.

Though he was facing his mother, he never looked up. "The queen will— She'll—*oh!* Then I won't move there."

He snatched up a tiny piece and held it suspended above the chessboard. "I'll move... I'll move..." He stared down at the board. "I'll move... umm..."

"That's check and checkmate, son," the man said quietly. "Any place you move, you move into danger."

But Jeffie had already moved into danger—had been placed in terrible danger by this meddling stranger! For three long years, since the death of her husband, Coffee had kept Jeffie safe from chess. She'd thrown out every chessboard in the house, had locked all the scrapbooks of Richard's victories away in the attic along with his trophies. She'd forbidden Maureen, Richard's own mother, from even saying the fatal word in Jeffie's presence. And now this stranger had opened the door she'd thought she'd locked forever. He had no right! No right to do that, no right to hunt them down and invade their privacy. No right to remind them of things better forgotten and buried. As Coffee crossed the room, she was trembling.

"No!" Jeffie wailed suddenly. "I'll move—I can— I can—" His small face screwed into a knot of rage and desperation.

"You can't, son," the man said softly. "You're licked." He held out his hand for the piece that Jeffie waved. "But you played one heck of a game."

"No! I can—"

Coffee dropped to her knees beside him. "Jeffie..." Her voice was shaking so badly, she stopped and tried again. "Jeffie... where's Gram?" She caught his arms and pulled him gently to his feet, already knowing the answer to her question. In the small, safe town of Jackson, New Hampshire, children were granted a degree of freedom unknown to city kids. Maureen must have gone to the grocery store, and Jeffie must have chosen to stay behind. "Where's Gram?" she insisted anyway.

He hadn't even heard the question, she realized as he turned dazed eyes her way, eyes of that same palest blue that Richard's had been. At the look in them, Coffee felt as if a hand had curled around her heart and squeezed tight. He looked at her as Richard had looked, those first few times after they'd married, before she'd learned never to interrupt him while he played chess. He looked lost, stunned, trapped halfway between two worlds, belonging to neither. "Mommy, I've gotta—"

"You've got to go to your room, Jeffie," she cut in with a brittle gaiety that was belied by her trembling hands. "I want you to do your homework now. We're going down to North Conway tonight to see a movie." Standing, she urged him toward the door, but he resisted her, leaning back against her hands and turning to stare at the board.

"I've gotta *move*—My king's—"

"No, Jeffie, forget the silly game." He dug in his heels, but she pushed him forward. "Now run and do your homework. I'll be up in a few minutes to check it for you." She propelled him out the doorway.

"No!" He spun around and tried to reenter the room, but she caught the door and pulled it against her side, blocking his way and his view.

"Yes." She put all of a mother's weight and authority behind that single word, and gave him a look to match. "Right now, young man. Upstairs and get busy. March."

"*No...*" Tears of frustration glittered in his eyes. But at least that lost look was gone—he was back in her world. That was what counted.

"Go," she said again. "I'll be there in a minute."

He went, slowly at first, staring incredulously over his shoulder at her, then, when she didn't relent, he broke into a run. She listened to him pounding upstairs, his angry sobs knifing into her, then she drew a shaking breath, turned around and shut the door firmly behind her.

As her eyes locked with the stranger's, his black, thick brows lifted in an expression that might have been surprise, might have been ironic amusement. But otherwise, he didn't move. He simply sat, his big hands relaxed on his knees, those dark eyes not missing one freckle on her face.

"Out!" she said, then didn't trust herself to say more.

"You're Mrs. Dugan." His voice was deep, but not smooth. It had a husky roughness to it that grated on her nerves.

"No kidding, Sherlock! Now take your game and get out of this house before I call the police. You're trespassing."

"No, I'm not." Except for a slight narrowing of his dark eyes, he didn't move. "Your son invited me in."

"Well, I'm inviting you out! *Now!*" Swooping to her knees beside him, she grabbed the hinged board, spilling the chess pieces onto the rug. She flipped it over to expose the hollow underside where the pieces would nest, then scooped up a handful of the chessmen and threw them inside.

"Now?" He grinned suddenly. "You're not going to tell me to *march,* like poor Jeffie?"

She had gathered a second handful of chessmen while he spoke. As his taunt sank in, her hand clenched around them till their sharp edges hurt her fingers. He was laughing at her, mocking even the pet name she called her son. But that was mere insult compared to the injury he'd done them already—he'd brought chess back into their lives when she'd thought they were safe at last. If she'd dared, she would have thrown the chessmen in his face. Instead, she drew back her hand as she swung toward the fire.

"Hey!" Fingers clamped around her wrist, stopping the throw in midair. "No, you don't!"

She'd got up on her knees to make the toss. As he swung her back to face him, she fell forward, catching her weight on her free hand. She bit off a cry as her palm came down on a chessman. The piece snapped and a sharp edge dug into her. With the pain, her impulse to destroy died.

He must have thought she meant to grab more pieces to throw. With a snarl, he caught that hand as well and lifted it, holding her half-suspended before him by her wrists. Breathing hard, they glared at each other.

In the firelight, his eyes were coal black, touched with fire. They were too close to her own. Coffee wriggled, trying to back away from those tiny flames, but his grip only tightened until she could feel the thud of her pulse beneath his fingertips.

"I'm pretty attached to this set," he growled finally, when she didn't speak. "My dad gave it to me."

She'd forgotten the strength in a man's hands. Was that what flooded her eyes with tears, or was it the memory of Richard, giving Jeffie his first chess set for his fourth birthday? She dropped the chessmen she'd been holding and turned her head aside. "I'm sorry," she muttered. "That was stupid of me, but—" But there was no way she could explain to this stranger all the pain, all the— She shook her head, shaking the regrets aside; they were not to be shared with a stranger.

He lifted her slightly, then set her down to one side, away from his precious chessboard. His hands gentled on her wrists, but he didn't let go.

All she wanted to do was wipe her eyes, but she was too embarrassed to demand her freedom. She looked back at the fire, refusing to meet his gaze.

His thumbs brushed idly across the soft undersides of her wrists, and she sucked in a startled breath. She'd forgotten the touch of a man's hands. That thrill of electric awareness as if her skin were warm velvet and he was stroking its nap the wrong way. But why did it have to be this intruder who reminded her?

Abruptly he let her go. "My name's Dodge Phillips, Mrs. Dugan."

She knuckled her lashes, her cheeks, then trapped her hands between her knees and looked up at him. "I don't care who you are. Why can't you people just leave us alone? No comment means *no comment*—don't you understand plain English?"

"You people?" He returned her glare blankly. "Who do you think I am?"

"You're from *Time Magazine*, or *People*, or *Newsweek*," she murmured. "Or *Sports Illustrated*, or *Yankee*, or *American Chess*." Listing the magazines, she saw all their swarming, hard-eyed reporters again, and her own voice hardened. "You want to know the inside story—what really happened to Richard Dugan and why, and how I feel about it, in disgusting detail. Where's your rotten camera—you're missing the perfect photo op. His grieving widow in tears. Isn't that what you came for?"

"No." He shook his dark head, frowned and swiped at a lock of hair that had fallen over his brow. "Not exactly..."

"Not exactly? Then how about a shot of Mount Washington, where he died? Or his grave? Everyone settles for that when we won't talk to them. I'll even give you directions to it." Anything to get him out of the house. Anything at all to break the hold of those dark eyes. With a jerk of her head she looked down to find his chessmen still scattered on the carpet.

She picked one up, glanced up at him warily, half expecting him to pounce on her.

He smiled—he knew exactly what she was thinking—and pushed the chessboard across the rug to her. She set the chessman inside the box and shot him a defiant look.

"I knew your husband, Mrs. Dugan," he said quietly. "I played against him a time or two."

The shock of that registered in her hands—a nasty little jolt of electricity starring out across her palms, then sizzling up her wrists. She hunched her shoulders and picked up another chessman. "Get out of this house," she said softly, not meeting his eyes.

For the first time, his voice held a note of exasperation. "I'm trying to tell you that I'm *not* a reporter. I don't work for a magazine, nor for a newspaper. I'm a chess grand master myself, rating 2520, if that means anything to you."

A squeak of half-hysterical laughter escaped her lips. He thought that made things *better?* With genuine amusement lighting her face, she glanced up at him, reflexively checking to see if he shared the joke, then shaking her head as she realized that, of course, he wouldn't. She looked down again, found a rook hiding in the shadow of his big foot and picked it up.

No, that didn't make things better. It made Phillips a different sort of enemy. He wasn't one of the probing, sensationalist outsiders, trying to package someone else's grief and sell it to a celebrity-mad public.

He was one of the insiders—one of the elite of the chess world, with a rating like that. Just another of the fanatics who had lured Richard into their dark, seductive world of combat and obsession. Death in miniature, meted out on a black-and-white checkered battlefield. "Go away, Mr. Phillips. I don't want to talk to you about anything." She dropped the two pieces into the box, then scanned the rug for more.

Phillips pulled the inverted chessboard to him and began ordering the jumble of chessmen, fitting each into its proper niche. Coffee breathed a sigh of relief. He was going, then.

"I've talked to your father-in-law," Phillips said without inflexion.

She shrugged. "I've never met the man." Nor would she ever want to. If anyone had made Richard what he was...if anyone had killed the man she loved... And then John Dugan hadn't even bothered to come to the funeral.

"Yes, I know you've never met." Phillips's big hand caressed his neatly arranged pieces. "You're the other half of Richard Dugan's life. It was split right down the middle, wasn't it? The chess world...and you."

Yes, that was precisely right. She looked up at him defiantly. But it wasn't something she was going to try to explain to a stranger.

Yet defiance was one thing. Holding this man's gaze was another. To do so was to open herself to him, somehow. To suffer his gaze moving across her face like warm, delicately questing fingers. To feel him peering into her eyes, as if he'd cupped his hands and leaned close to peer through a reflective window. Coffee had too many secrets to guard to permit that intrusion.

Her breath coming a little ragged, she looked away, found one final chess piece lying at the edge of the rug. When she picked it up, she realized it was the white king. But the tiny ivory cross that should have crowned its head was broken off. This was the piece she'd crushed by accident.

"Looking for this?" Phillips picked the fragment of cross off the carpet with an ironic grimace and held it out to her.

She didn't take it. "Chess—one thousand. Me—one." She murmured the score, trying to make a joke of it, then regretted it immediately. This set had meant something to Phillips, after all.

His lip curled suddenly. "You hate it that much?" He plucked the broken chessman out of her hands with none of the gentleness he had shown before. "Is that what happened to your husband, Catherine Dugan—you tore him in half? You forced him to choose between you and the game he loved? Is that the kind of woman you are?"

No, that wasn't what had happened. Whatever choices Richard had made, he had made alone. That was the way he had lived. The way he had died. Even if she would have wanted that kind of influence over her husband, he had never granted it. Had never let her close enough.

But to explain that, she would have to explain everything, would have to tear off the bandages and show this man where she hurt. "Who—who are you to judge?" she whispered, her throat aching with the strain of the words.

"I'm your—"

Down the hall, the front door opened with a crash that made them both jump. Thinking of the door's decorative panels of glass, Coffee winced again and turned toward the sound. A woman's high giggling and a young man's shout of laughter followed the crash, then one pair of booted feet scampered up the stairs, accompanied by more giggles. The honeymoon couple was home.

"Hey, honey!" Sam Daley called from the hall. "What about our tea?"

From above, Jennifer Daley trilled a reply that Coffee couldn't catch.

"Okay," Sam replied, then the sound of his heavy footsteps started down the hall toward the kitchen.

With a sigh, Coffee rose and looked down at Dodge Phillips. "I have to serve my guests their tea, Mr. Phillips. Can you show yourself out?"

As their eyes locked, she thought he was going to ignore her dismissal. Then his mouth twisted into a grim smile.

"Certainly." He dropped the king into its niche, started to close the case, then stopped, looking down at the pieces. Coffee frowned. What was he staring at now? But before she could figure that out, he grinned, surprising her with a flash of excellent white teeth and a wonderful crinkling of the outer corners of his dark eyes, and shut the box.

A knock sounded on the family-room door. "Hello? Anybody home?"

Coffee swung around. "Coming, Sam."

While she bustled around the kitchen, Coffee kept her ears tuned to the hallway. He had said he would go, but if Dodge Phillips was leaving the house, he was certainly light-footed. She sliced the brandied fruitcake, a specialty of the inn, then lifted her head at the sound of the front door opening and gently closing. *Good.* She shut her eyes for a moment in heartfelt gratitude, then started as the whistle of the teakettle announced that the water was ready for the teapot.

Pouring the water into the flowered pot, she bit her lip. She had to go to Jeffie and soon. How long had he been upstairs alone? The interview with Phillips might have lasted minutes or much longer. There had been something so upsetting, so disorienting about his dark eyes, that their time together hadn't been measurable in the normal way.

But then, nothing about the encounter had felt normal. Her blood was still rushing like a stream tumbling down the mountainside.

And I still don't know what he wanted, she realized suddenly. She'd been so frantic to see the last of him, she hadn't thought to ask. *Doesn't matter,* she told herself firmly. After the reception she'd given him, he wouldn't be back. Now if she could only repair the damage he'd done...

She dropped the tea egg into the pot, put the lid in place, then paused, her eyes darkening. Jeffie had not played a game of chess in three years, not since his father's death. And yet, with Phillips's encouragement, it had all come back to him in an hour or two, apparently.

She shuddered, rattling the cups on the tray as she lifted it. The rules of chess weren't easy. Each piece had a different way of moving and attacking. Most seven-year-olds couldn't master the rules of the game at all, and yet Jeffie had learned to play at four. But then, Jeffie was no ordinary child. That was the whole problem.

And I'd almost managed to forget that, she told the absent Phillips bitterly, *until you came along.*

With the tray balanced on one arm, Coffee opened the rear door to the large room that looked out over the steep hillside and down to the brook below. This room was a combination lounge and dining room, with two large tables for family-style dining at the end near the kitchen, and several couches and chairs grouped round the big fireplace at the other end. And it was empty. Coffee clucked her tongue in exasperation. If the Daleys didn't want their tea, then why—

"Coffee?" Sam Daley hovered in the doorway at the far end of the room. "I was wondering—" He shifted his weight from one size-twelve shoe to the other and back again. "Would it be okay if we took our tray up to the bed—" At the word, he suddenly, wonderfully, blushed scarlet and half turned away, then swung back and finished in a rush, "—to our room?"

She had to fight back her smile as she brought him the tray. "Sure, that would be fine." She thought regretfully of the white medallion bedspread on their big fourposter—it would show every spot of dribbled tea—then resolutely shoved the worry aside. What were honeymoons for, after all? She handed over the tray, then followed him into the front hall and stood there while he loped up the stairs. She'd give him a moment to make good his retreat before she followed him up to Jeffie's room.

Jeffie... She swung to look out through the etched and beveled glass panels of the front door to the parking area before the old farmhouse. Phillips would be long gone, of course, but—

But he wasn't. With a gasp of dismay, Coffee stepped close enough to the door to chill her nose against its glass.

Bent nearly double, Phillips leaned down, his hands braced on the open window of Maureen Dugan's car. Coffee's mother-in-law was smiling up at him and nodding at whatever he was saying. Clearly they were already on the best of terms.

Unable to take her eyes off the pair, Coffee groped blindly for the door handle. First he'd revived Jeffie's memories of chess, and now he was charming Maureen. What had Richard called such an attack—a pincer play? And just what did this man want, anyway? She would have to find out.

But as she yanked open the door and stepped into the glassed-in vestibule, Phillips moved back from the car. With a cheery wave, Maureen drove on through the parking lot and around the side of the house. She would bring the groceries through the garage door into the kitchen. Coffee paused, her hand on the storm door. Still shaken from their last encounter, she had no desire to confront Phillips again. Maureen had probably learned what he wanted. Coffee could always ask her instead. And most likely it was merely curiosity.

While she dithered, Phillips had crossed the snow to a small, low-slung black car—a Porsche. It figured, Coffee thought. The car matched the man's arrogance and sleek power. Her hand dropped away from the doorknob. He was going; was as good as gone. Why stop him now?

And then, as he opened his door, he glanced back at the house. Coffee took a step backward, but he wasn't looking her way. His square chin was lifted. As she watched, that same grin, a smile that made her own lips automatically twitch in response, flashed once more. Dodge Phillips raised his right hand and flipped a casual salute at whoever watched him from above. Still smiling, he folded himself into his car.

And suddenly she knew. He'd been waving to Jeffie. Jeffie must have climbed up into his dormer window on the third floor, must be staring after the man like a puppy left behind by its master as Phillips backed the Porsche around in a curving K-turn.

A shaft of pure terror shot through her. Phillips had reopened the Pandora's box of Jeffie's terrible craving for chess. What if she could not shut it again? Coffee wrenched open the door, bounded across the wide porch and down the front steps. The Porsche was backing toward her. As it stopped and prepared to move forward, she rapped the car's sleek side.

Phillips's head snapped her direction. He shifted to neutral, then pressed a switch that rolled down his window. "Yes, Mrs. Dugan?"

Fear for Jeffie clawing at her soul, she could hardly find words. "St-stay away from my son!" she stammered, and gripped the cold edge of his window. "Do you hear me?"

His face hardened. "I hear you, but that might be difficult. Your mother-in-law invited me to stop by for lunch tomorrow." His eyes swept beyond her, scanning the inn. "I understand she owns this place?"

So he *was* trying a flanking attack. Coffee saw her own knuckles whiten where they gripped the glass. "Yes, she does. But understand this also, Mr. Phillips. Maybe I can't stop you from coming here." Though she would try—oh, would she ever try! "But you are not to talk to my son. You are not to play chess with him—ever."

"It's too late...Coffee." His dark eyes probed her face. "Can't you see that? It's in his blood. You try to lock that talent up inside of him, and Jeff's going to explode."

Coffee. He had called her "Coffee." Few people outside her closest friends and family knew her nickname. And now this stranger, a man who was voicing her deepest, darkest fear, and smiling while he did so. "Who *are* you?" she gasped. "Just who do you think you *are,* butting into our lives this way?"

His smile lost all its warmth. "Pretty lady...I'm your late husband's biographer." Clad in black leather, his fingertips grazed her knuckles. "Now watch your fingers." The glass rose between them as she snatched her hands away.

Richard's biographer. Coffee closed her mouth slowly as the Porsche growled out of the parking lot. But there had never been a biography written of Richard Dugan! Phillips's car turned downhill toward the valley and shot over the narrow wooden bridge that spanned the river. Above the rush of the water, she heard its planks grumble, then go silent. The car vanished beyond the dark pines, swallowed up by the twilight.

Or did he mean— Her heart stumbled, then steadied as she brought a hand to her chest. Did he mean that he meant to *write* Richard's biography? "Oh, no, you *don't,*" Coffee whispered aloud. "No, I can't let you do that, Dodge Phillips!"

She spun on her heel, took a step toward the house, then remembered to look up. The dormer window of Jeffie's room was empty, but its curtains still swung gently to and fro, to and fro.

CHAPTER TWO

"JEFFIE?" COFFEE TAPPED a finger on his third-floor bedroom door. When he didn't answer, she opened the door slowly. "Jeffums?"

His little room was in darkness. Four squares of silver gray marked the window from which he'd watched Phillips leave. The only other thing catching the light was Jeffie's pale hair where he lay sprawled on his bed, face buried in his pillow.

"Hey, kiddo." She sat down beside him, spread a hand between his bony little shoulder blades and felt him tense. Crying or mad at her or both? But he wasn't shaking. Mad then. She breathed a silent sigh of relief. His anger was easier to take than his hurt, somehow. She rubbed his spine with the heel of her hand, up and down a few times, but he didn't relax.

What to tell him? How to explain, without telling too much? Though he'd outgrown the stage when she and Maureen had called him the Why-Why Bird, he was still fond of the question, and she didn't want to get into whys. Not for years and years yet. "You wore your shoes to bed, big boy."

"Don't care." At least that's what the muffled growl sounded like.

"Well, let's take 'em off, shall we?" When his consent didn't come, she took them off anyway, slipping off first one sneaker, then the other. As she grasped each of his ankles in turn, she remembered when she could encircle one with thumb and forefinger. No longer. He was growing so fast.

She dropped the shoes beside the bed and went back to rubbing his spine. ''Did you start your homework, Jeffie?''

He growled something unintelligible and hunched his shoulders.

But the answer was apparent when she glanced at his desk, the top of which was bare. He hadn't touched his books—not that there'd be much to do. She sighed. He wasn't going to make this any easier. ''We can't go to a movie till you do your reading, kiddo.''

''Don't care!''

Sulking was not something Coffee normally encouraged, and it seemed best in this crisis to act normally. ''Now listen, big boy,'' she said firmly.

''You didn't listen to *me!*'' he turned his head to point out, then swung back to muffle a hiccuping sob in his pillow.

''No. . .'' A pang of guilt shot through her. ''I guess I didn't.'' She rubbed him some more. ''Was there something you wanted to tell me?''

''I won.''

For a moment, her ears refused to make sense of the growl. Her brain didn't want the translation.

When she didn't respond, Jeffie rolled onto his side. ''I won the first game,'' he said clearly.

Deep in her stomach, fear spun down and around in a cold, sucking whirlpool. How many games had they played? And could Jeffie have really won, or had Phillips only let him think so? Not that it mattered. What mattered was the exultance that sang in her son's voice when he said it.

''I would'a won again if you hadn't stopped me,'' he assured her, his voice taking on that hard edge of bravado that meant he knew he was lying. He was still at an age where he thought that, if he said something firmly enough, it would come true.

"Jeffie, I want you to listen to me and listen good." She rocked him gently in time to her words. "I don't... want...you...playing that game. Do you understand? You're not to play that game. *Ever.*"

"It's called chess," Jeffie told her on a note of clear defiance.

Dear God, so he had a name for it now, thanks to Phillips. And what he could name, he could ask for, at school, in a toy shop.... Stalling for time and wisdom, she leaned to switch on the bedside lamp. "It doesn't matter what it's called, I don't want you playing it. Is that clear?"

"Why?" It was more challenge than question, the way he delivered it. His bottom lip stuck out and his brows drew down in an exaggerated scowl.

"Because I said so." She didn't utter those words often. She'd hated them as a child, and she always wanted to laugh at herself when she was driven to use them. But not tonight. There was nothing funny about this crisis. "And I don't want you...seeing that man again. Understand?"

"His name's Dodge."

"I don't care what his name is, I don't want you talking to strangers!"

"He knew my dad."

Coffee opened her mouth, then shut it again as guilt swept over her. Did he miss having a father that much, that he could be captivated instantly by anyone who'd known Richard? She'd tried so hard to strike a balance between Jeffie's natural curiosity and her need to conceal. And she thought she'd found a good compromise. There were pictures of Richard all over the house, and she always answered Jeffie's questions. He knew who his father was.

But he'd never asked her *what* Richard had been, or why he'd died. She'd hoped those hard questions wouldn't come for years and years. And they shouldn't, if Phillips hadn't set him wondering.

"All the same..." she said, stymied by her child's logic. "Maybe he knew your father, but I don't know *him*. So I don't want him in this house, and I don't want him playing games with you. Is that understood?"

Gold lashes drooped over his ice blue eyes, and his pout deepened. Coffee bit back a sigh. Most of the time, he was a sunny, cooperative child, but when he caught a case of the stubborns... She touched his snub nose. "You understand me," she said with more authority than conviction.

Eyes still closed, he wrinkled his nose and tossed her hand off. Uncertain what else to say, she studied the rest of him. He was still wearing the flannel shirt and jeans he'd worn to school this morning. He'd lost a button again, off a sleeve this time. She often teased him about the Button Monster, who hopped along behind him, amassing a collection of Jeffie buttons. "What have you got in your hand, kiddo?" she asked, noting the clenched fist below the gaping sleeve.

"Nothin'..." He wriggled, then hid his fist under his pillow.

Normally she wouldn't have made an issue of it. A child needed his privacy, especially a male child living with women. But some instinct tonight... "Let's see it, Jeffie," she said firmly.

His blue eyes opened and studied her with—there could be no other word for it—wariness, an emotion she'd never been offered before in their relationship. She forced her mouth into an encouraging smile. "Show."

His hand crept back into view and came to rest on his stomach. Small, grubby fingers uncurled to show her a tiny chessman. The black king.

Her heart seemed to stop cold, then start with a terrible jerk. She remembered Phillips, and his sudden grin as he'd looked down at his assembled chessmen before closing the case. He'd known the king was missing, and yet had said nothing. *He wanted Jeffie to have it!* There was a roaring in her ears, and it was more than the distant hum of Owl Brook, but she forced a note of calm into her voice. "Give me that, Jeffie."

His fingers closed tightly, and the king vanished. "It's mine." He might have been claiming a birthright, not just a bit of ivory.

"It's Mr. Phillips's, and he'll want it back." But he didn't. He'd wanted Jeffie to have it. He'd passed his terrible gift to her child right under her nose. "Give it here and I'll see he gets it."

"No."

"Positively *yes.*" There was no compromise on this one. No way she could let him keep that piece and brood over it, as Richard had done with his chessmen. She slid her arms under his body and scooped him off the bed—no easy task nowadays, but in this moment of fear, he seemed a featherweight. "Now we're going to put it away, and that's that."

"No!" He arched his back and kicked his heels, but ignoring that, she lugged him out of his room and across the hall to her own.

She scanned the room and decided, then carried him over to the tall, bird's-eye maple bureau in the corner. "We'll put it in the drawer here, where it'll be safe till I can get it back to him. Okay?"

"No!" He kicked his legs again. "Let me down!"

"Not until you put it away." She pulled out one of the little lingerie drawers at the top of the bureau. "You can put it in there." Her back was starting to ache. Propping the elbow that supported his shoulders on top of the bureau, she looked down at him, her face set with determination. She'd stand here till her back broke in two if she had to.

And he must have seen it in her face. His own started to screw up and redden, and his lips to tremble. "It'll be safe there," she said coaxingly. From him most of all. And he from it. "Put it right there on that lacy thing. That's a nice place for it."

Tears were starting to stream now. She wanted desperately to hug him, needed badly to put him down. She shifted her weight and stood fast. "You can't keep it, baby. Mr. Phillips...Dodge...will want it back. *That's* my good guy," she said softly as he dropped it on her camisole. For a moment they both stared at its stark elegance, nestled in a bed of frothy white lace. The image of Phillips's firelit face flicked through her mind and the skin on her wrists crawled where his hands had held her. She shivered, bent her knees and set Jeffie on his feet. "That's my big boy." She tried to hug him, but he wrenched away. Heart aching, she stood by the bureau while he ran out of the room, then his door closed with a bang.

She stood listening for a while, and though she couldn't hear him through the walls, she knew he was still crying. And that he wouldn't take her comfort for this one. Biting her lip with the pain, she turned back to the bureau. "Damn you!" she whispered, looking down at the black king.

She closed the drawer, shutting it out of sight. But for neither her nor for Jeffie was it out of mind.

NORMALLY COFFEE BAKED for the week on Friday, so that the house would smell wonderful for the weekend guests. But tonight she needed an outlet for her restlessness. She poured the last measure of whole-wheat flour onto the batter and stirred till it stopped sticking to the walls of the bowl.

"I just don't see what good can come of seeing him," she said to her mother-in-law across the kitchen.

Maureen looked up from stacking her supper plates in the dishwasher. "Maybe you can't, Coffee, but where's the harm?"

Phillips was dangerous in so many ways, Coffee went speechless trying to sort them all out. He meant harm to Jeffie, and somehow, in a way she could sense but not explain, he meant harm to herself. She shook her head in frustration and turned the dough out onto her floured kneading canvas. "He just wants to root around in our lives, Maureen. Why do you have to indulge his grubby curiosity?"

"There was nothing grubby about the man. He was perfectly pleasant." Maureen shut the dishwasher with her hip, then wiped a wisp of white hair off her broad forehead.

"Of course he was! People are always pleasant when they want something." Dusting her hands with flour, Coffee attacked the dough.

"Well, if he wants something from me, he has something to trade," Maureen said tartly. "He knew Richard. And he wants to talk about him."

Which is more than you do. The unspoken accusation hung in the warm kitchen air between them. Flushing with shame, Coffee looked down at her kneading fingers. Maureen was right; she didn't like to talk about Richard much. She had so much guilt tied up with his memories. When she opened the door to them, everything came avalanching down on her at once. All the things she should have done, could have done, might have tried. And though she knew in her head that she'd done the best she could for Richard, she couldn't seem to feel that in her heart. There was always this gnawing pain that she must have left something undone. That she'd missed something...had failed to turn some key to his heart or his mind or his happiness.... And so rather than suffer the pain, she kept that door closed.

How would I feel? she wondered, as she flipped the sticky dough and sifted a little more flour onto it. *How would I feel, if I'd lost Jeffie and then no one would let me talk about him?* "I'm sorry," she murmured and glanced up at her mother-in-law. "But..." But there was still Jeffie to think of. She hadn't been able to save Richard from himself, but there was still Jeffie. And this time she would beat the game, whatever it took.

"I hated the reporters as much as you did," Maureen reminded her. Crossing to the big stainless-steel refrigerator, she pulled out two pounds of bacon and carried it over to the range. "But Mr. Phillips didn't seem pushy like that. And a biography of Richard, that's not like a magazine article that gets thrown out with the next trash...." She laid the bacon out piece by piece on the griddle. "You know, sometimes I think that people might just forget that Richard... ever lived."

"Oh, Maureen!" Coffee cried in protest. Folding the dough over, she thumped it with the heels of her hands. "No one will forget Richard, *ever.* He made his mark. They'll dissect his games for the next hundred years."

"His games, yes. But the man?" Maureen asked softly.

The anguished, driven, ruthless man who had been her husband, Jeffie's father, Maureen's remote but beloved son? Coffee folded and pushed, folded and pushed. Was he someone that anyone needed to remember or know but the people directly involved? Whose business was that dark side of Richard but their own? Sure, it would make a biography more fascinating—milking the tormented-genius angle—but...

She shook her head. "Maureen, I've got my own son to think about. I don't see how reading a book like that will ever make Jeffie feel good about his father. I'd rather he got his picture of Richard through you and me, not from some stranger's interpretation of the facts. Not from some gloating distortion. I don't want him reading a book like that—ever."

Maureen turned the flames of the griddle up slightly. "You know, you can't hide Jeffie away from chess forever, Coffee. One day he's going to want to know everything about his father. Everything about the game."

"But not in his formative years!" Coffee cried fiercely. "I've told you that. If he catches the obsession at this age—" She picked up the bread dough and slammed it down. She was overkneading it, but she couldn't seem to stop. In her mind's eye, she could see the photos in Maureen's scrapbook, hidden away in the attic. Richard at eight, in his first tournament, scowling at a chessboard. Richard at nine, a ring of adults staring raptly down at his board while the grown man he was beating gnawed at his cuticle. Richard at ten, unsmiling as he held up a trophy as big as himself. There was not one picture in that scrapbook of Richard smiling. *Not one.* "Maureen, I'll do whatever I have to do, to let Jeffie grow up normal, to keep him away from that horrible game. If that means leaving you, leaving this town—" Fleeing that damned, prying Phillips...

At her words, Maureen swung around. She crossed her arms over her solid body and lifted her square Yankee jaw. *"Go ahead,"* she said distinctly. "Go ahead and take my grandson away from the only home he's ever known! I'm sure that's the best thing. Cut his roots, throw away his friends, leave me to run this place alone...."

The two women glared at each other across the room. Tears glittered in Maureen's eyes, and Coffee could feel a sympathetic prick in her own. With her white hair and her raw bones and her defiant stance, Maureen might have been a settler of three hundred years ago, braced on her door-step, holding the marauding Indians at bay. The image made Coffee smile in spite of herself. "Now you're fighting dirty," she pointed out. Even with both of them, Owl Brook Inn was a handful. Maureen couldn't manage the bed and breakfast alone. "Next you'll be telling me you're over sixty and your old bones ache in the mornings."

Maureen's mouth twitched reluctantly. "I was getting to that," she admitted, her voice gruff with emotion. She spun around and picked up an egg aimlessly, then set it down again.

"You know we're not going to leave you," Coffee told her rigid back. "Not just because this is Jeffie's home, but because you've made it mine. I can't forget that, Maureen. Not *ever*. But—" She stopped as the swinging door to the hallway swung inward.

Hair rumpled, Jeffie stood there, dressed in his pajamas. "I'm hungry," he growled.

"I should think so," Maureen agreed.

He had not come down for supper, and Coffee had not permitted his grandmother to take a meal up to his room as she had wanted to do. But it looked like a small boy's stomach had beaten out pride once again. Coffee breathed a little sigh of pleased vindication, and carefully avoided Maureen's eyes. This was no time for "I told you so's".

"How about a bacon-and-tomato sandwich?" Maureen suggested as she bustled to the refrigerator.

Jeffie considered, looking as if he'd like to find fault with that suggestion, but his stomach settled the matter with a loud rumble. He nodded stiffly, and Coffee coughed to hide her laughter.

Not being in the doghouse, Maureen could chuckle aloud. "You can eat it in front of the fire, all right?"

Maintaining his dignity, Jeffie nodded and shuffled off to the family room. As soon as the door closed behind him, the two women giggled.

"I'm sorry," Coffee said finally. "I'm way out of line. You see whoever you want, Maureen." She'd been an idiot to think she could ever dictate to her strong-willed mother-in-law. Might as well try to move Iron Mountain, once Maureen had made up her mind. And her pride and stubbornness had run in a straight line from her, to Richard, to the child in the next room.

"I'll make sure he's long gone by the time Jeffie gets home from school," Maureen assured her as she spread mayonnaise on bread.

"Thank you," Coffee said, accepting the tacit apology. "But there's one other thing, Maureen."

The older woman clucked in irritation. "Isn't there always?"

Coffee ignored that and pressed on. "Richard was your son, and of course you can talk about him all you want. But Jeffie is mine, and I don't want him in this biography. So will you promise not to discuss Jeffie—or me—with Phillips?" If he was seeking the personal angle for his book, then perhaps limiting the available material would change his mind.

"You're being silly," Maureen snorted. She completed Jeffie's sandwich and set it on a plate.

"Maybe so, but there it is," Coffee told her flatly. And she would make herself scarce as lilacs in January, come lunchtime tomorrow. The last person in the world she wanted to meet again was Mr. Dodge Phillips.

BUT THOUGH SHE MIGHT AVOID the man, Phillips still had the power to turn her world topsy-turvy, Coffee discovered the next morning. She stared into the lingerie drawer where the black king had been tucked the night before. *Gone.* She prodded the camisole where the chessman had rested, as if it might have burrowed undercover during the night. But of course it wasn't there.

"Jeffie!" she whispered in disbelief. This wasn't like him at all. He'd known the piece was off-limits. She'd made that clear enough to him.

Shutting the drawer with numb fingers, she stood, trying to marshall her spinning thoughts. This was Phillips's fault. She hadn't had a moment's ease since he came to town. That dream last night… Waking with pounding heart and twisted sheets, she hadn't remembered much of it, only dark, fire-lit eyes moving near and then nearer to her own, until she fell into their darkness. *That dream and now this.* It was his fault.

Crossing to her son's room, she stood dithering in the doorway for a moment, then changed her mind. No, she couldn't search his room. She'd simply have to demand the piece when he came home from school.

Running in her socks down two flights of stairs, she found Maureen in the kitchen. "I can't find his chessman after all," she said briskly, keeping her worries to herself. "If you'll ask Phillips for his address, I'll mail it back to him right away."

"All right." Maureen glanced at her curiously, but apparently decided not to ask what the problem was now. She turned back to the tomato quiche she was making.

Making a fuss for Phillips's lunch, Coffee nodded wryly. Hadn't anyone ever told her that real men didn't eat quiche? "I'll be back by two," she muttered. She stalked into the sunroom and stepped into her ski boots.

TWENTY MILES OF PERFECT snow worked its usual magic on Coffee's worries. The day was cold and clear, with a tang of pine each time she inhaled. She climbed the Wildcat Valley Trail until she could branch off toward Black Mountain, then circled its peaks by way of the Woodland Trail. Though the next day the slopes would teem with weekend skiers, she had them nearly to herself that Friday. She passed no one she knew.

By the time she returned to the Owl Brook Trail, she had put her fears behind her. As always the mountains reduced man-made problems to their proper proportions. And she'd been making a mountain out of a molehill with Phillips.

So she'd dreamed about him...so what? After three years alone it would have been more surprising had she *not* dreamed after such an explosive and close encounter with an attractive male.

And her larger fears for Jeffie were just as exaggerated. So Phillips had talked about writing a book—that didn't mean one would be written. In her twenty-six years, Coffee had noticed that roughly every third person she met meant to write a book—someday. But somehow, no matter how they talked, they never got around to doing it.

And Phillips certainly hadn't looked like a serious writer to her. He wasn't the bookish sort at all, not with his keen eyes and those big, competent hands. So this talk of a bi-ography was probably a whim, or an excuse to come knocking at the shrine. Maureen would have satisfied his curiosity by now and have sent him on his way. Coffee could mail his chessman back to him, and in time—a short time, she prayed—Jeffie would forget all about this. Life would go back to normal. "It will," she promised herself as she stepped out of her skis, below the sunroom. It absolutely had to.

Still she entered the house almost on tiptoe, her ears pricked for the rumble of a masculine voice. And she breathed a sigh of relief when she found only Maureen sitting in the family room.

Her mother-in-law sat in her favorite chair before the fire. She was working on the quilt that always lay close to hand.

"He's gone?" Coffee asked without preamble.

Maureen looked at her strangely. "Left an hour ago," she said, around a mouthful of pins. She looked back down at her work.

"Good." Coffee beamed with satisfaction. "Did you get his address for me?" That was the one bit of unpleasantness remaining, she remembered. She'd have to relieve Jeffie of the chessman as soon as he came home. Glancing at the clock, she frowned. Come to think of it, where was Jeffie?

Maureen took the pins out of her mouth. "He said he'd let you know, as soon as he found a place." She looked up expectantly.

"*Found* a place? You don't mean in Jackson?" Coffee dropped down on the sofa as if someone had kicked her behind the knees.

"Yes. He plans to stay in town while he researches his book. He said he'd be looking at Elsa Warner's cabin, this afternoon."

"No," Coffee said flatly, and popped back up again. Not possible. The Warner's little rental chalet was less than a quarter mile down the hill, just off the trail to town. Why, Jeffie skied past that cabin almost daily. He'd be returning up that trail any time now, since he'd skied to school this morning. "He can't do that!" She hurried to the phone across the room. "*She* can't do that!" Elsa Warner was a friend, after all.

"I don't know why not," Maureen countered. "This *is* America."

Coffee gritted her teeth and dialed. Then shifted from one boot to the other while the Warner's phone rang and kept right on ringing. She cradled the receiver. "Elsa's probably showing it to him right now." She started for the door, then swung back again. "Can you handle things for the next hour?" The first weekend guests should be arriving any time now.

"I expect I can," Maureen said dryly. "But if you think you're going to change that man's mind, you'd better think again."

CHAPTER THREE

THE WARNER'S RENTAL chalet was perched on the mountainside a hundred feet above the trail that led down to Jackson. Coffee turned off the main track onto the ungroomed private path that zigzagged up through tall pines and white birches to the cabin's deck. The back of the chalet could be reached by road, but as was often the case in Jackson, that was the long way around. And she had no time to waste.

As she herringboned up a steep rise, she noted absently that someone had passed this way before her. Most likely an exploring tourist. She blinked as she passed from the cool blue light of the woods into a sunlit grove of head-high Christmas trees. The Warners had cleared enough forest to make a view for the cabin above, and being thrifty, they had planted the slope in balsam fir for extra income. She sucked in the lovely holiday scent and slogged on.

Looking up, she could see the cabin's deck jutting out from the hill above her, and beyond it, the peaked roof of the little A-frame. A wisp of smoke trailed out of its rough stone chimney. *Oh, no.* At the sight of occupation, her already racing heart thumped harder. No, this simply couldn't be happening.

But someone had cleared the snow off the wooden steps that led up from the hillside to the elevated deck, Coffee noted as she stepped out of her skis and leaned them against a support piling. Someone with very large feet had broken a short trail from the bottom step to the cords of wood stacked under the deck. She froze suddenly, her scanning eyes transfixed by a footprint to the left of the big ones. This one was smaller, too small to be an adult's. With a gasp, she swung toward the stairs.

A pair of short, waxless skis leaned against the stair railing. Jeffie's ski poles, with their Garfield the Cat decals pasted to the shafts, rested beside his skis.

Fingernails biting into her palms, she stood still for a moment, struggling against her first impulse, which was to tear up the stairs and snatch Jeffie from harm's way. *Be cool,* she thought desperately, taking a deep breath. *Easy does it.* She jumped, then glanced up at the sound of a sliding door opening somewhere overhead.

Feet tramped onto the deck. "One more load should do it," Phillips stated in his husky baritone.

"I'm gonna carry five this time," Jeffie announced.

"Don't need that much, buddy. The bin's almost full. Carry two or three logs, and that'll be great. You've been a real—" Phillips's voice halted abruptly. He stopped short on the top step, his hands braced on the railings at either side. "Mrs. Dugan," he said. His voice had lost its vibrant note of amusement. Now it was warily neutral.

Easy does it. Mounting the stairs with the gliding deliberation of a climber crossing an ice bridge over a bottomless chasm, she kept her eyes locked on Phillips's.

His dark brows drew together slightly, and he backed away. Automatically, he put out a hand to steady the child who stood behind him.

At the gesture, Coffee's heart sank. Maybe it was because his hand remained on Jeffie's shoulder. The gesture was almost possessive. *No, you can't have him. I've given one to chess, I'll not give another.*

As she climbed the last few steps, she came into Jeffie's view. His small mouth rounded into a guilty O.

So he remembered what she'd told him the night before. She couldn't remember when he'd last disobeyed a direct order. Could the pull of chess be that strong? Or was it simply male companionship that was the attraction? But Jeffie had never tagged after Peter Bradford, when the ski patrolman came calling at Owl Brook Inn. "Jeffie." She kept her voice calm, though the effort hurt her throat. "What are you doing here?"

"Umm…" The boy's clear skin flushed rosy pink and he stole a glance up at the man beside him. "Uh…"

Returning Jeffie's glance, Phillips patted his shoulder, then let him go. He looked back at Coffee and crossed his arms. His expression had shaded from neutrality into something harder.

"I brought back his king," Jeffie muttered. He glanced up at Phillips again, then crossed his own arms. "Dodge needs it to play chess," he added with more assurance.

A wave of desolation swept through her. Her son was mimicking this—this stranger. And she was shut out. The two of them had closed ranks against her, masculine recklessness resisting feminine concern. She felt outnumbered, stunned that Jeffie could so easily shift his allegiance. But *she* was right—that was what she had to keep on remembering.

"Well, now that you've returned it, we need you at home," she said, and was surprised at how normal she sounded. "The fire needs laying in the guest lounge, and then Gram wants help in the kitchen." Later she would think what to say to him concerning this disobedience, or perhaps it was better to simply ignore it. Right now, she simply had to get him away from here. "So scoot, big boy, and tell Gram I'll be home in a minute. I have to talk with Mr. Phillips.''

Jeffie opened his mouth to protest, then shut it again. The request was plausible, after all. Coffee and Maureen had made him feel a part of their team since he could toddle, and in the last year or so he had become a real help to them. He knew he was needed. Still, his eyes darkened with disappointment, and he glanced up again at his tall companion.

But if he was hoping Phillips would countermand his dismissal, he was disappointed. The man gave him a lopsided smile and a brisk clap on the back. "Good to see you again, Jeff."

Ignoring the man beside her, Coffee moved to the railing to watch her son trudge down the stairs, then step into his ski bindings below. Jeffie glided off down the slope without a backward glance, not bothering to use his poles, and disappeared among the Christmas trees.

When he was gone, she could contain herself no longer. She spun from the rail, her hair flaring out around her shoulders. "I told you to stay away from my son!"

Across the deck, Phillips stood at ease, his arms crossed, his dark eyes intent on her face. Without changing his stance, he shrugged. The constrained movement made her suddenly aware of his forearms, bare below the rolled up cuffs of his red flannel shirt. Beneath the dark swirls of hair, they were pure muscle, surprisingly tan for this time of year. "So you did," he agreed. He turned toward the sliding glass door that led into the chalet. "Cold out here."

Did he think they were going to end the conversation just like that? Startled, she balanced on the balls of her feet for a moment, then lunged after him. He had not closed the door behind him. She slammed it shut to announce her entrance and glared around her.

The bottom floor of the A-frame was airy and open. The living room in which she stood offered spectacular views out over the deck to the southern mountains. Its cathedral ceiling heightened the sensation of spaciousness, and the fire leaping behind the glass door of a big wood-burning stove gave it warmth. In the small but nicely laid out kitchen beyond an intervening butcher-block bar, Dodge Phillips turned the flame down beneath a whistling teakettle.

"You can't rent this place," she said, crossing to lean against the bar and scowl at him.

He laughed—a short bark of amusement that didn't sound so amused. "I already have." He opened a cabinet, shut it and opened another.

"Elsa Warner's a friend of mine," she told him, letting the threat hang in the air between them.

"Good. Then don't make trouble for her. She's accepted my money already, and she couldn't turn me out if she wanted to. Which she doesn't." He turned and smacked two mugs down on the counter before her. "Hot chocolate or coffee, Coffee?" His lips quirked, then straightened again.

He had one of those intensely masculine mouths, the kind with almost no upper lip visible. An oddly sensitive line divided the gold, clean-shaven skin above from the rather full and beautifully carved lower lip. "Who told you my name? Maureen?"

"Your husband." His dark, clever eyes registered the shock on her face, then he turned to rummage in a grocery bag. "In Berlin. We were drinking espresso at the time."

Eyes stinging, she swung to stare sightlessly out at the mountains. Somehow she'd never pictured Richard discussing her with anyone. She'd always assumed that she didn't exist for him, when he was off on a tournament. Behind her she heard the small clinks and stirrings of beverage making, then a thump as he set down a mug by her elbow. She smelled instant coffee. "I wanted hot chocolate," she said perversely.

He laughed again, under his breath. "Ask for it next time." He came around the bar, holding his own mug, and walked over to check the fire.

She didn't bother to tell him there'd be no next time. He knew it already. "How did Jeffie know you'd be here?" she asked, his back to her as he opened the glass doors and shoved in another log.

In profile, his lips curved again as he studied the flames. "I gather it was something along the lines of Elsa Warner stopping at the post office when she left here, and seeing someone who has a kid, who knows a kid, who knows Jeff. I hadn't been here thirty minutes when he showed up."

So Jeffie had not taken the chessman to school with the intention of returning it to Phillips. Had he taken it along for fear she'd search his room for it, or simply because he couldn't bear to be parted from it? Either reason was equally disturbing. "I don't want you seeing Jeffie again," she told him.

"It's a small town. I'm supposed to avert my gaze when we meet on the street, Coffee?" He turned to look at her mockingly.

"You know what I mean."

"I know what, but not why," he agreed. He stood and prowled toward her. "If you're so dead set against chess, why does Jeff know how to play it at all?" He stopped and stared down at her, his eyes narrowed.

She was still propped against the bar by her elbows. To straighten would put her nose-to-chest with him, but to stay there, leaning back like that, left her feeling vulnerable, too open to his probing gaze. Her skin tingled with his nearness, felt again like ruffled velvet as his eyes moved over her. But if he was trying to intimidate her, she was not about to let him see it was working. She tipped back her head to look him in the eye. ''Richard taught him. Jeffie hasn't played since he died.''

''But that's—'' A slow, beautiful smile spread over Phillips face. ''That's three years ago.'' He shook his head wonderingly. ''He'd forgotten a few of the moves, but once I showed him, he took off like a rocket. Attacked with two pieces—that's the surest sign.''

''Sign of what?'' she asked, though she knew already.

''Of genius—chess genius, that is.''

She shivered. Richard had said the same once, the last time he'd played Jeffie. She remembered the look on his face when he'd said it. It hadn't been this look of pleasure that Phillips wore, it had been a look of...fear. But whether it had been fear *for* Jeffie, or fear *of* him, she hadn't known. Hadn't dared ask. Whichever, he'd never played his son again, though Jeffie had begged him. And it was a month after that that he'd set out for Mount Washington. She shivered violently.

''Cold?'' Phillips brushed her arm with his knuckles.

She flinched away from his touch and drew in her breath sharply. ''No.'' What was she doing, standing so close to this man? She had the feeling that an immense stretch of time had passed while she'd stood there remembering. If she wanted to remember, she should remember that this man meant to write a biography about Richard!

And what if he mentioned in his book that Richard Dugan's son showed the same signs of precocious chess genius that his famous father had? How long would it be before someone read that, and told Jeffie about it? She could picture Jeffie reading the book himself at age ten—he was reading well above his grade level already. She could imagine him coming to her, a fanatic gleam in his eye as he asked her if he was really a chess genius. She shook her head with a jerk. No, ten was too early. If she could protect him until he was fifteen... But how could she protect him at all, with this man practically living in their back pocket?

Her eyes came back into focus, and rose from his broad chest to his quizzical face. As their eyes locked, she felt a twinge of pure panic. It was her dream all over again. He was too near. *"Move,"* she said crisply.

His brows lifted, but he moved back a step. She pushed off the bar and started across the room.

"Going so soon?" he asked ironically.

She wheeled to face him, but kept on moving away. "I help run a bed and breakfast, and it's Friday afternoon. Yes, I'm going." Her hand touched the glass of the door behind her and she stopped. "But I want you to promise me—"

"To shoot myself at the first available opportunity?" he mocked.

It hit too close to home. She felt her eyes go round and she spun toward the door. But she was standing too close to it— her knuckles smashed into the glass. She gasped with pain and the expectation of disaster, but the glass didn't shatter. Trembling, she brought her bruised knuckles to her mouth.

Hands closed on her shoulders from behind. "What did I say?" Phillips demanded, his breath tickling her ear.

"Nothing! J-just stay away from my son. Don't talk with him and don't play chess with him." She shrugged her shoulders, but he didn't let go. If anything, his grip tightened. She closed her eyes, trying not to shiver with his touch, feeling each individual fingertip that pressed into her flesh—her thin sweater was no protection at all.

She took a deep breath and forced her eyes open. She could see his reflection dimly in the glass, making one shape with her own. "You're really writing a biography of Richard? Seriously?"

"Yes." His hands slid a few inches down her arms, then back up again.

"How long are you staying here?" She put an edge to that question.

His laugh was rueful, seductive, warm on her ear. "Long as it takes to gather the facts, Coffee. So if you want me out of town that badly..."

"Yes?" Reaching down, she slid open the door, and the outside air chilled her face. It was a welcome antidote to the warmth at her back.

"You ought to cooperate," he said softly, and let her go.

Coffee shook her head and walked out. She didn't look back, not once. But somehow she knew he was watching, standing unmoved and unmoving in his doorway, till she'd reached the protection of the little pines.

THE AFTERNOON AND EVENING passed in the usual Friday flurry. The inn was half-full of guests by the time she returned, and more soon arrived. Maureen and Coffee hurried upstairs to show guests to their rooms, and downstairs to greet new arrivals at the door. There was the big punch bowl of mulled cider in the guest lounge to be filled and refilled, the fire to be fed and poked to a cozy blaze. There were the guests to be introduced to each other and jollied into some sort of sociability around the hearth and the TV set. There were the constant and familiar questions to be answered: Where could one get an extra-special meal in town? Where could one find a reasonable meal? Which were the best trails for beginner cross-country skiers? Which offered the most scenic vistas or the most thrilling descents? When would Coffee give the two-hour skiing lesson that was part of the basic weekend package?

Around eight, the worst of the rush was over. Most of the guests had gone out to find their dinners, reasonable or outrageous, depending on their budgets. The rest were amusing themselves in their own rooms or in front of the TV set in the lounge. In the kitchen, Coffee set a tray of empty teacups near the dishwasher and straightened her back with a sigh. Maureen turned from the range to give her a weary smile. "Where's Jeffie?" Coffee asked. She'd seen him only in passing for the last few hours, and she hadn't had a second's peace to think what she'd say to him.

"Up in his room, I think." Maureen stirred the pot of stew that would be their own supper. "Supper in ten minutes, if you want to tell him."

"Sure." Coffee started for the stairway, then stopped at the registration desk as the phone rang. "Owl Brook Inn," she said automatically, and glanced toward the front door. Light from a pair of headlights swung across the glass insets as a car pulled into the parking lot.

"Coffee? This is Joe Harris," the owner of the Blue Duck Inn said briskly. "I've got a walk-in couple here, and we're full up. You don't have a double left, do you? Something on the nice side?"

"Not this weekend, Joe. We've got one teensy room with one teensy window in the back, bathroom down the hall. It's half price, but then it's only half size. We rent it when we're desperate."

"Not their style," the innkeeper said regretfully. "Guess I'll try the Village House."

As she hung up, the storm door opened, and someone paused out in the vestibule. Through the decorative glass panels of the front door, Coffee could make out white-blond hair and blue eyes staring in at her. The outline of the person seemed humpbacked and strangely distorted, but that must be some trick of the swirling patterns on the etched and frosted glass. She smiled hospitably, but the person simply stood there.

Coffee crossed to the front door and opened it. "Please come in," she said. "We don't keep it locked."

Two pairs of huge blue eyes looked into her own. A blond young woman held a blonder two- or three-year-old balanced on her rounded hip. The little girl's head nestled on her mother's shoulder. The child had the blank, accepting look of a dreamer just awakened. Her mother smiled hesitantly. "This is the Owl Brook Inn?"

"Yes, it is." As she must surely know. The gilded and carved sign that hung by the entrance to the parking lot could not be missed. But perhaps she didn't read English? There was a faint but unmistakable accent to the woman's words. "Would you like to come in?" Coffee held the door wide in invitation, though she looked at the drowsy child with concealed dismay. With their antique furnishings and adult clientele, most bed and breakfasts took a dim view of renting rooms to guests with young children. In spite of Jeffie's residence, the Owl Brook was no exception.

"Please." But the blonde entered the house the way a tiger hunter enters the bamboo grove, eyes wide and constantly scanning. She turned in a half circle, taking in the hall, the big staircase, what she could see of the guest lounge, then turned back to Coffee.

While she'd been making her inspection, Coffee had taken a look at the parking lot, then closed the door. No one seemed to be waiting out there. So these two were traveling alone? She found those search-beam eyes aimed at her face again.

"I would like a room for the night," the blonde said with quiet determination.

She was German, Coffee guessed, or perhaps Swedish. But she didn't look like a skier—too softly rounded, and few people brought a child skiing, anyway. So what was she doing here? Jackson was not on the way to anywhere. "I'm afraid we only have one room left," she shook herself out of her speculations to say. Quickly she explained about the little room, and stated its price for one night.

The blonde gasped, then blushed a charming shade of rose.

"I know it seems high," Coffee agreed, "but this is tourist country, on the weekend, when everyone's rates go up. And I can guarantee you it's the cheapest room you'll find in town." She smiled sympathetically. "You know, there are motels with cheaper rates down in North Conway. I'd be happy to call around and find a room for you, if you like."

The woman rested her cheek against the child's downy hair for a moment, then straightened and shook her head slowly. "No, we are very tired. It took much longer to drive here than I thought."

Where did she mean by here? The Owl Brook? Jackson? Almost without thinking, Coffee reached out to draw a fingertip down the child's velvet-soft arm. "Look, it *is* late. I'll knock the rate down twenty dollars if you want to stay here tonight. And tomorrow we can help you find something that suits you better."

"You're very kind." While Coffee filled out the registration card for her, the woman switched the child to her other hip. Her name was Anke Meier, and her home address was Cologne, Germany.

"You've come a long way!" Coffee observed cheerfully.

The blonde did not return her smile. "Yes."

She was in no mood for chatting, Coffee decided, discarding all questions as to what the woman was doing in this part of the world. "This is your key," she said, "and I'll show you your room as soon as you like."

"My luggage..." Anke Meier looked dazedly toward the parking lot and half turned in that direction.

She was dead on her feet, Coffee realized, coming quickly around the desk. "Look, you've got your hands full. Could I hold her for you while you get your bags from the car?" She held out her arms for the child.

The woman hesitated so long that Coffee thought she'd made a mistake of some sort. Embarrassed, she started to drop her hands and step back, when suddenly the woman nodded.

"If you would." Gently she tranferred the clinging child to Coffee's arms. "Her name is Brigitta. Gitta..." she broke into German, a crooning reassurance that was clearly a promise to return.

"Nein, Müttie!" the little girl protested, but she didn't struggle.

"Hi, there, Gitta. Mama will just be a minute now." Her arms full of the satisfying warmth and weight of the child, Coffee sat down in a chair across from the desk. "You've had a long drive, huh?"

Brigitta swiveled in her arms to meet her gaze and study her with eyes bright with intelligence. Coffee's words clearly held no meaning for her, but they must have been reassuring all the same. The child relaxed against her like a sleepy cat. With a half-guilty glance toward the door, Coffee bent her head to sniff the child's hair. She could have closed her eyes and believed it was Jeffie, almost; they had the same smell of sunshine, like a sheet fresh from the clothesline. She sighed happily. Nice to hold a baby again. Jeffie was growing less and less willing to be cuddled as he grew older. A pity. She looked down at the child's drooping, incredible lashes, then jumped as Maureen spoke.

"Now what have you got there?" She put her hands on her hips.

Coffee looked up mischievously. "Gee, can I keep her, Ma? Please? Huh?"

Maureen shook her head in amusement. "That would just about give you a matched set, wouldn't it?"

Coffee nodded, smiling down at the child. The door opened, and Anke Meier stepped inside, lugging an enormous, battered old suitcase and a carryall full of baby gear. She set the suitcase down almost on her own foot as she saw Maureen.

Coffee rose and came forward. "Maureen, this is Anke Meier, from Germany."

Maureen's hand had come up automatically as Coffee spoke. Halfway horizontal it froze, missing by inches the hand Anke had extended. Maureen's eyes widened, then she blinked rapidly.

Coffee glanced at her in surprise, then quickly looked down again as Gitta nearly toppled out of her lap. Stretching out her fat little arms, the child reached for her mother with a demanding cry. Coffee jiggled her up and down, then looked up to find Maureen and Anke shaking hands, their eyes locked on each other. A wavering smile crossed Anke's pale face. Maureen looked almost grim.

"You're staying here?" she demanded.

"I put her in the rose room," Coffee interceded quickly as Anke nodded. What was bothering Maureen—the thought of a child in the house?

"Then I'll show them up," Maureen continued on that same harsh note. She held out her hands for the child, and still wondering, Coffee handed Gitta over.

But if Maureen didn't like children as guests, she still loved children. As Gitta settled under her chin, her face relaxed for a second and a smile flickered. Then she stiffened and led the way up the stairs. "I'll send Jeffie down," she called back to Coffee. "And the salad needs dressing."

Eyebrows raised, Coffee stared after the procession for a moment. Between the suitcase banging against her legs and the big carryall, Anke had her hands full, and for a second Coffee considered offering to help. But both of the women seemed to have forgotten her existence, and somehow she felt she wouldn't be welcome. A strange feeling, in her own house. *And just your imagination,* she told herself as she headed for the kitchen. Phillips had rattled her cage two days in a row, and now she was seeing bogeys around every corner.

But she didn't want to start thinking about *him.* Determinedly she switched her thoughts to her own son, and just what she was going to do with him. In spite of his disobedience, she didn't want to ground Jeffie. That would be making too great an issue of it. She was still praying that his fascination with Phillips would fade, given time and distance.

So instead, I'll keep him too busy to play outside this weekend, she decided. They'd turn out his bedroom, wash the walls. Then, if he had any energy left, they'd drive down to North Conway, get him those new sneakers he'd been needing. She wrinkled her nose. *Who am I kidding? I'm the one that'll run out of energy!* Starting toward the kitchen, she stopped short as she caught the first bitter whiff of burning stew, then she broke into a run.

CHAPTER FOUR

KEEPING JEFFIE OCCUPIED indoors wasn't easy at the best of times. But this weekend, Coffee thought, the task seemed even harder. Everyone was on edge.

She knew what was making her own stomach churn with anxiety—she'd seen Dodge Phillips's Porsche that morning. It had been parked in the village when she drove down to pick up rental skis and boots for the guests who'd be taking her lesson at ten. Luckily she hadn't run into its owner, but the car itself seemed as menacing as a black knight poised to pounce on an unsuspecting white pawn. So that accounted for her nerves.

But what was bothering the normally cheerful Maureen? "Jeffie, I think I've had about all the help I can take," his grandmother grumbled. "If you're going to be Mr. Butterfingers this morning, maybe you better go somewhere else." She picked up the chunk of Swiss cheese that Jeffie had dropped on the kitchen floor and ran it under the faucet.

"Can't." Jeffie shot a look of rebellion at his mother, who'd just come in through the sunroom. "Mommy said I have to help you." He turned back to the pile of grated cheese on the chopping block before him and began pushing it into a checkerboard pattern.

"Well, thank you very much, but if you're going to play with the food, I'd rather do it myself." Maureen picked up his board and whisked it away.

"Why don't you go read a book, kiddo?" Coffee suggested, ruffling his hair.

"Read 'em all," he growled. Shaking her hand off, he climbed down from his chair at the kitchen table.

"Ohh, I'd bet there's one or two you haven't tried yet. And there's a new *Ski Magazine* in the guest lounge." Coffee sneaked a puzzled glance at Maureen, who was whipping eggs as if her life depended on it.

"That stupid baby's in there," Jeffie said wearily. He might have been explaining that the lounge was full of cobras, as any fool should know.

Coffee hid a smile. A good night's sleep had made a world of difference in the cuddly child of last night. This morning Brigitta had been more of a circus than twelve monkeys and a raccoon tied tail to tail. Anke Meier was doing her best to ride herd on her child, but lacking a leash or ankle irons, there was only so much vigilance one mother could bring to the problem. Gitta's experiment with what happens when one pulls on a tablecloth—with the table set and ready for breakfast!—had been the crowning disaster so far. Luckily only a few other guests had been down for breakfast by then, and they had been more amused than bothered by the incident. But poor Anke had been mortified and close to tears.

And Maureen certainly had not been entertained. Perhaps that was the source of her bad mood. "Come with me and I'll find it for you," Coffee suggested, tacitly offering her protection.

The baby was indeed in the lounge, seated with her mother in the window seat overlooking the brook. Anke was reading to her from a children's book, but she looked up as Coffee and her son entered the room. Her expectant expression faded to one of vague alarm. "We're just looking for a magazine," Coffee explained and headed for the side table near one of the sofas, with Jeffie practically treading on her heels.

But if they had a reason for being here, what was Anke doing? she wondered. Why travel all this way to plant one-self in the lounge of a ski resort? The day was a dazzle of sunlight on snow outside, and yet here she sat. She hadn't mentioned staying a second night and yet she was making no move to leave.

"Here it is," she said, and handed the magazine to Jef-fie.

"Gitta, *nein!*"

Coffee looked up to see Brigitta making a beeline for Jeffie, her starfish hands outstretched, her face alight with glee. "Now here's someone of the *proper* size!" her expression seemed to say.

But Jeffie didn't agree. Drawing himself up to his full four feet, he pointed a finger at the child. "No!" he roared.

On she came, giggling. With a groan of despair, Jeffie took to his heels and bolted out of the lounge, Gitta in tod-dling pursuit.

"*Nein*, Gitta, *nein!*" Anke caught her daughter near the door, swooped her up, then turned to look at Coffee. Both women broke into laughter, smothering their giggles as they glanced guiltily toward the doorway.

Across the hall, the door to the family room shut with an emphatic thud, and that set off another round of giggles. Coffee came forward to smooth the child's silky head. "Poor Gitta," she chuckled. "Come back in twelve years or so and he'll run the other direction, I promise." She looked up to find Anke had lost her smile. She was staring at her blankly.

Lost something in the translation, Coffee decided uneasily. She considered explaining, then discarded the notion.

"Well, I've got to give a ski lesson," she said instead, and sidled toward the door.

As LESSONS WENT, THIS ONE was a success. All of her six pupils had cross-country skied at least once before, and they made rapid progress. Coffee started them in the field to the side of the inn, and once she was sure they could handle a gentle slope, she took them down to the Eagle Mountain fields beside the Wildcat Brook. After an hour they were doing so well she escorted them down the "more difficult" Yodel Trail into the valley. They took a few spills on the way, but came up smiling. "Good snowplow, Mrs. Beamis!" she called from her position alongside the trail. "Bend your knees a little more, Mr. Mello. *That's* it."

They arrived on the Wentworth golf course winded and flushed with triumph, new converts to the gentle pleasures of ski touring. Their lesson was over and now they could ski to their choice of restaurants for lunch in the village. Quickly Coffee dispensed last-minute advice, congratulations, and recommendations as to lunch spots, then waved them on their way.

Except for her two young hotshots—a pair of lawyers up from Boston. Joe Halloran looked up from the map of his ski-trail guide. "The Ellis River Trail is over that way, Coffee?"

"Yes, hook around those trees and then straight ahead."

He nodded, satisfied. "We're going to ski upriver to the Dana Place for lunch. Want to come?"

Her smile wavered in spite of herself. "Thanks, but I'm afraid not. I can't leave Maureen with all the chores back at the house." She had not skied the Ellis River Trail for three years. Maybe never would again. Richard had gone that way, on his way up to the Gulf of Slides.

She left them with a wave and headed back across the golf course toward her trail uphill.

The track passed close to the graveyard and Coffee glanced toward Richard's grave as she glided past. A red-jacketed figure stood before his stone, dark head bowed as the man read the inscription. Her left ski came down outside the groomed furrow of the track, and Coffee stumbled. She caught her balance and looked sideways again, to find the man watching her. Dodge Phillips. She should just keep on skiing. He couldn't follow her through the snow without skis. She'd be safe.

But warring with her impulse to flee was a simmering outrage. This was *her* town—must she fear meeting him wherever she went? The man was ripping her peace to shreds simply by being. She stepped out of the trail and slogged through the unmarked snow toward the black iron fence that separated the graveyard from the surrounding fields.

Phillips tromped through the snow to meet her, gloved hands jammed in the pockets of his ski jacket, breath trailing white over his shoulder. His eyes flicked over her face, and his smile of greeting uncurled. "Coffee," he said evenly, and rested a boot on the bottom rung of the fence.

Now that she was here, she didn't know why she'd bothered. There was no use telling him to get out of town again. Looking at his resolute jaw, she suspected few people successfully told this man anything. And after the start they'd gotten off to, it was a little late for pretty pleases.

"Now you say, 'Hello, Dodge,'" he instructed gravely. "Or if you're really feeling extravagant, you could try, 'How's it going?'"

Some other place or time, under other circumstances, she could have liked this man. She felt a smile trembling inside, or maybe that was just terror. Something about him scared her even as it attracted.

"And then I say, 'It's going rotten,'" he continued when she didn't speak.

"Why?" The question popped out before she knew she even wondered.

"Because nobody will talk about your husband, that's why. I mention his name and they either look blank, or they clam up and stare over my shoulder. What's everyone hiding?" he asked with a hint of frustration.

That was the last thing she wanted him to think—that there was some secret waiting to be dug up. He looked like the type who would dig to China, if need be. Stubborn, curious, intelligent—those were dangerous traits in someone who meant to write Richard's biography.

She brushed her hair back behind one small ear, then dropped her hand as his eyes followed the movement. "No one's hiding anything. It's just that those who knew Richard know I don't like him gossiped about. The rest didn't know him." She looked toward the white marble stone, its shoulders iced with snow. It looked like a chessman, keeping cold and eternal guard, yearning for a black foe to venture forth and give battle.

"Richard didn't talk to people much." His interest hadn't been people at all. People couldn't be picked up, moved, set to one side of the chessboard, and Richard had never quite forgiven them for that. Any of them. Certainly not her. She shrugged.

"But he grew up here, he had to have had friends."

Did he? Apart from herself? She glanced at Phillips, then looked away again. "He was only here summers, starting when he was fourteen—after Maureen divorced and moved back here. I think if he had friends, they were all involved in chess. People he knew in New York City, where he lived winters with his father, or from the tournaments."

Phillips leaned forward to rest his black gloves on the fence between them, bracketing her own. She looked down at his gloves. He had big hands; she liked that in a man. Such hands promised strength, protection, a safe haven for a woman. She jerked her eyes back to his face as he spoke. "He didn't have friends in chess, Coffee. He had opponents."

She shivered and looked away across the graveyard. *Yes.* That was why she'd do anything—anything at all to keep Jeffie away from chess.

"Did *you* know him?" Phillips challenged, his voice soft and harsh all at once.

Had she ever really known him? She swung to stare over her shoulder, but from down here in the valley, the dark, fir-clad slopes of the lower mountains shut off all views of Mount Washington to the north. But always, that craggy peak reared high in her mind, its icy gales ripping off a plume of sunlit snow. If she'd known Richard as she should have, she'd have known he didn't mean to come back that day. She'd have known to stop him. She jumped violently as Phillips's glove closed over her mittened fingers and squeezed. She swung back to face him.

For a moment they simply stared at each other. There was something besides curiosity in his narrowed gaze. Coffee gulped and lifted her chin. She didn't need his pity, if that's what it was.

But she must have misread him, for his next question offered no quarter. "If you knew him, then do you know why he quit chess? What would make a man walk away at the absolute peak of his success?"

Once again she saw the snow-shrouded peak. *That* was where his talent had led him.

"He never played another game of chess after he took the world championship in Berlin, did he, Coffee? I can't find anyone who gave him a game in the eight months he lived after that. Why would he turn his back on the thing he did best in all of life?''

She swallowed convulsively, but still her words came out ragged. ''Maybe he just grew tired of it. He'd proved he was the best in the world. He'd reached the—the top. What more was there?'' What more in life was there for him?

But there should have been more, her heart protested. There'd been herself, and Jeffie, and Maureen, and this world of such sparkling beauty it almost hurt to look at it. Why couldn't that have been enough for him?

''Tired of it?'' Phillips snorted incredulously. ''Did Baryshnikov tire of ballet, after he'd danced *Swan Lake?*''

Startled, she opened her mouth, then closed it again. Was that how he saw chess? Two players dancing a joyous pas de deux, rather than two enemies locked in a duel to the death? Richard had been known for his killer instinct, his relentless aggression. But for what had this man been known, while he was earning his grand master points? ''Why do you have to write this book?'' she blurted suddenly. ''Surely there are other people to write about? Why don't you go write about Baryshnikov, or... or...'' Or anyone but Richard.

He laughed aloud. ''You think that's what I do for a living? That I'm a professional biographer?''

''You're not?'' she asked stupidly.

''No.'' He smiled again at the thought. ''I write educational software. Computer games that teach logic to school children. You've never heard of The Lady or the Tiger series?''

Numbly, she shook her head. But her astonishment was giving way to outrage. If he wasn't doing this for the money, was he doing it for the fun of it? Was he raking up things best forgotten, or never known, as a gentleman's hobby?

Reawakening Jeffie's terrifying thirst for chess on a whim? "Then...then if you're not, what do you think you're doing, trying to write Richard's biography?" she erupted. "What makes you think you're even qualified to write it, if you're nothing but a silly amateur?"

Clearly, he wasn't used to having his competence questioned, and just as clearly, he didn't like it. His brows snapped down and he leaned forward across the fence, his jaw jutting aggressively. "Oh, I'm qualified, all right, Coffee. I know the chess world inside and out—that's one advantage I have over a professional biographer. And I was there in Berlin, as a second to Haley, and as a commentator for the networks. And I'll put my prose up against the writing of any pro you care to compare it to. Not that I need your permission to write this book."

"Lucky for you, since you'd not get it!" With a bitter shrug, she took a V-step away from the fence. She was wasting her time here.

But reaching across the fence, he caught her wrist. "Coffee!"

Her hair whipped in a fine golden arc as she swung back to glare at him.

"Since I'm going to write this book whether you like it or not, wouldn't you prefer it to be accurate?" His black, leather-clad thumb stroked the top of her mitten. "Without your help, I may get some of the facts wrong. Doesn't that worry you?"

"No." No, what worried her was that he'd get the facts *right*. That somehow he'd guess Richard had not simply lost his way on the brutal flanks of Mount Washington, as had so many other winter travelers. That he'd not lost his life, but had abandoned it as not worth living. She didn't want Jeffie to read that in a book, ever. He wasn't going to inherit his father's legacy of despair if she could prevent it. "No, you can't blackmail me that way, Mr. Phillips."

His brows shrugged, then he actually smiled. "Was worth a try."

She looked down pointedly at his detaining fingers. "Now, if you don't mind, I should go."

"Certainly." He let her go. "And would you remind Maureen that I'll be dropping by shortly, to pick up that scrapbook she promised me?"

"You can't stop by today!" she protested. "Jeffie's there."

His mouth twisted. "Send him out to play, if you think I'm contagious."

And where would Jeffie go, if she sent him out to play? Straight down to Phillips's cottage?

When she didn't speak, he shook his head wonderingly. "What are you so afraid of?"

"Nothing." Nothing she could tell him about, for fear he'd tell the world.

His dark eyes probed her face. "Why are you so afraid of *me?*"

"I'm not!" But she was. As she started to shiver, she swung away again, hiding the spasm with the movement. In the distance, she saw a familiar figure in a yellow parka—it was Peter Bradford. The trail patrolman was headed toward Yodel. Cupping her hands to her mouth, she hallooed, then waved when he spotted her. She glanced over her shoulder at Phillips. "Got to be going," she said. "That's a friend of mine."

As opposed to me, his dark eyes said ironically.

Yes, her own answered. She gave him her sweetest smile, not meaning a bit of it, then turned and slogged off through the snow. When she reached the trail, she settled into her gliding stride and almost flew toward Peter, as if he were the one point of stillness in a world gone spinning out of control.

FIFTEEN MINUTES OF UPHILL work and Peter's cheerful company did little to soothe Coffee's ragged nerves. Maureen knew that she meant to keep Jeffie away from Dodge Phillips! So what did she think she was doing, inviting the man over on a weekend? And given Maureen's strange mood of this morning, did Coffee dare express her displeasure, or should she simply grit her teeth and endure the situation? Meanwhile, what should she do with Jeffie? She'd have to distract him in his room somehow until Phillips had come and gone. Leaning her skis in the mudroom, she slipped out of her ski boots and stalked sock-footed up the stairs into the sunroom, her blue eyes ablaze with exasperation.

"No, Anke," Maureen's voice carried clearly from the kitchen. "You need that money more than I do. You pay me back some day when you can afford it, if you like."

Coffee paused halfway to the doorway as the words sank in. Tact suggested she not intrude on the scene taking place in the kitchen. She shifted from one foot to the other. So Anke Meier had not been able to pay for her room, even at the reduced rate Coffee had offered her last night. But then, why hadn't she said as much when the price was discussed?

"I do like," Anke said firmly. "As soon as I find a job..."

This sounded like a more positive note on which to barge in, and Coffee's feet were getting cold. She coughed, then came forward, treading heavily. When she stepped into the kitchen, Anke turned to face her, a high flush of pink along her wide cheekbones. Maureen also gave her an odd look, from where she stood by the kitchen table. The older woman held a rolling pin, and a white mound of cookie dough lay on the table before her. At her feet, Brigitta sat on the floor, fingering a key chain and humming a soft, two-note song to herself.

"Oh, hello, Anke," Coffee said casually.

The woman gave her a brief, taut smile and turned back to Maureen. "Well . . . I think we must go then."

"Yes, you should," Maureen agreed dryly. "And I have to get ready for teatime."

"I have only to get my bags," Anke said with great dignity.

Coffee flashed her a puzzled glance, then busied herself unwinding the wool scarf she wore. Anke looked almost hurt, but that made no sense. Why should she feel hurt, if Maureen had just given her a free night's lodging? Probably it was only embarrassment.

"Come, Gitta," Anke called. Then, when the baby ignored her, she gave a cluck of irritation and went to pull her to her feet.

Maureen dusted off her bony hands. "I'll mind her while you bring your bags down, Anke."

For a moment it looked as if the blonde would refuse the offer, then she nodded stiffly and left the room.

"Come on, big girl." Maureen hoisted the child to her hip and bounced her expertly. "Time for you to be going."

The child crowed something in German and jingled her keys in Maureen's face. Maureen chuckled, looked up at Coffee and lost her smile.

"Sorry I'm late," Coffee said uncomfortably. It was occurring to her that, if she was going to fuss at Maureen for inviting Dodge Phillips to the house, she couldn't exactly explain the reason for her own tardiness—that she'd stopped to chat with the man in question. "I'll start on the rooms as soon as I change clothes." Each of the guest rooms had to be spot vacuumed, given fresh towels. There were beds to smooth out and flowers to change in the vases. And then tea would be served in two hours.

"That's no problem," Maureen said, in almost a sing-song. "Take your time." Her attention had shifted back to Gitta, and it was to the little girl she was really speaking. Still jiggling the child, she strolled toward the hall and the front door beyond.

"But I do have a problem," Coffee murmured, with a wary glance toward the family-room door as they passed it. "I understand Dodge Phillips is stopping by in a little while?"

Maureen squared her jaw and kept walking. "Yes, he is, for a scrapbook I promised him."

"And just what am I supposed to do with Jeffie?"

Maureen swung to face her near the registration desk. "Coffee, you're making a storm in a teakettle, worrying about the man!" She stooped to set the child down, then crossed her arms and glared at her daughter-in-law. "You can't catch chess like a disease."

"Maureen, if you'd seen Jeffie when they were playing... The look in his eyes..."

Maureen shook her head stubbornly. "You can't blame everything about Richard on chess, my dear."

Oh, couldn't she? They'd had this argument before and had never yet reached agreement on it; weren't likely to this time. But still...

Maureen hurried to continue as Coffee opened her mouth. "I know Richard wasn't a normal—wasn't an easy man, but it wasn't only chess that made him that way. There was the way his father pushed him..."

A squeal of childish excitement caused both women to look around, and then up. Two-thirds of the way up the staircase to the second floor, Gitta clambered up another

carpeted step, her small bottom stuck high in the air, her
lace-edged panties peeking out from under her short dress.

"*No,* Gitta!" Maureen's reactions were the faster. She
leaped for the stairs and took them two at a time.

Coffee stopped with one foot on the bottom step. There
wasn't room for both of them on the stairway, and if they
panicked the child... The baby caught a baluster and pulled
herself to a standing position, then swayed backward on her
tiny, fat feet.

"No, Gitta!" Arms outstretched, Maureen reached for
her as the child wobbled and nearly fell. "You bad, bad—
oh!" As her foot slipped out from under her, Maureen
grabbed for the banister and missed.

"Maureen!" Coffee cried helplessly.

Arms flailing, her body toppled forward—landed with an
awful thud on one knee. Maureen cried out again, and
snatched at the balusters as she tumbled feet-first down the
stairs in a series of sickening little thumps.

"*Maureen!*" Coffee reached her as she stopped sliding,
three steps from the bottom. "Oh, *God,* Maureen, are you
all right?" She touched her back, smoothed a hand across
her bony ribs. "Oh, Maureen, say something!"

"What is it? What happens?" Anke Meier stopped short
on the landing above. As she saw Maureen's body, she let
out a shriek and dropped her suitcase. Gitta plumped down
on the stairs and started to howl.

"Don't move her!" a masculine voice commanded at
Coffee's ear.

Coffee glanced to the side, and found herself staring into
Dodge Phillips's dark eyes. He touched her cheek with a
fingertip. "She'll be all right," he said quietly, "but let's not
move her yet."

"Oh, Dodge..." Coffee blinked furiously—this was no time for crying—and turned back to Maureen. Up on the stairs, Gitta continued to wail loudly enough for them all.

CHAPTER FIVE

HOLDING TWO CUPS, Dodge sat down by Coffee in the emergency waiting room. "Hear anything yet?" he asked as he offered her one of the drinks.

Coming out of her daze, Coffee shook her head. "No, she's still in X rays." She focused on the cup before her, then accepted it. "Thanks."

"Sure." He settled back on the hard plastic couch beside her and draped one long arm over the backrest.

She had a lot for which to thank Dodge Phillips, Coffee reflected. He'd been like a rock back there at the Owl Brook, calming a half-hysterical Anke, helping Coffee revive Maureen and determine that nothing seemed to be wrong with her spine or hips. When they'd found that the medical rescue unit was out on a mission somewhere up on Black Mountain, he'd seconded her decision not to wait, but to take Maureen to North Conway themselves. So he'd carried Maureen out to the station wagon, then had driven her and Coffee down valley to the hospital.

And now he was simply lending his quiet support. His arm at her back radiated warmth. And Coffee somehow knew that should she give in to her dismay and curl into his shoulder, he'd be at no loss. He'd hold her as long as she needed him.

Bringing the drink to her lips, she found it was chocolate. She smiled a tremulous smile against its sweet warmth, then swallowed. He'd even remembered that. Slowly she settled back and felt her hair brush his arm. Tilting her face to the ceiling, she closed her eyes. *Be all right, Maureen,* she prayed. *You've got to be all right.* "She's older than she looks," she murmured, and bit her lip. "She's always been so strong, so independent...she'd *hate* it if that changed...."

The arm behind her stirred, then curved around her. Not even daring to acknowledge that he was there, Coffee sighed and let herself be gathered in. Coming to rest with her cheek pillowed against his shoulder, she kept her eyes closed. That was the only way she could pretend this wasn't happening and still surrender to the comfort she so desperately needed.

"It won't change," he murmured, his breath stirring the hair at her temple. "She's going to be all right."

Coffee smiled, and felt the tension start to seep out of her taut body. He couldn't know that, any more than she knew what the doctors would find, but it was what she wanted to hear all the same.

"You really care for her," Dodge added, his voice rumbling in his chest where her ear pressed against it.

She nodded. "I've lived with her ever since Richard and I were married."

"You didn't have a place of your own?"

She shook her head, her hair rasping softly against his flannel shirt. "We didn't have much money.... I was straight out of high school, and Richard only a year older... and he needed all the money he won in tournaments for travel to more tournaments, chess books—stuff like that. My folks had just moved to Florida, and they didn't... well, Richard and they didn't really..." She shrugged, dismissing that sore point. "Anyway, I wanted to stay in Jackson. I'd lived there all my life. So Maureen gave us the top floor of the annex. It has a kitchenette, everything we needed..." They could have been very happy there, if Richard had given them a chance. She squirmed restlessly, then felt Dodge take hold of her cup of chocolate.

"Done with this?" When she nodded blindly, he lifted it away—must have set it down on the side table.

"But he spent much of his time down in New York, being coached by his father and hanging around the chess clubs, didn't he?" Dodge continued. "I remember one snowy afternoon, about a year before he took the world championship, I saw him in Washington Park, playing with the chess bums on the benches there. He was playing five or six games at the same time, and those bums are some of the best players in the city, even if they're not rated. He'd bet them a dollar a game.... You didn't consider moving down to the city with him?"

If she had, would it have made a difference? She breathed a heavy sigh and felt his arm tighten in response, then ease again. "No...." Oh, she'd considered it, all right, but she wasn't a city girl. The one time she'd gone down to watch Richard play in a tournament, she'd hated it. Hated the noise and the danger and the dirtiness of the city, all those people crammed together, with no clean mountain air to breath. And of course, Richard's father had hated *her*. He'd been terrified she'd distract Richard just as his success was approaching its zenith. No, it had been better to stay in Jackson with Maureen where she was wanted and needed.

And once she'd become pregnant with Jeffie, she'd known her decision was the right one. She'd felt sure that to start a baby out right, you should surround yourself with beauty and serenity and the people who loved you. So she'd stayed in Jackson, hoping that one day, when Richard was done with his wars, he'd come home to stay, help her to build a real marriage.

"What about when Richard came to Jackson? What did he do to stay in training?" Dodge asked. "He didn't have a sparring partner up here?"

Coffee's eyelashes brushed his shirt as she opened her eyes. The arm around her no longer offered comfort, it felt like a trap. He'd been pumping her, hadn't he? She felt a hot stain of embarrassment spread across her cheeks. Here she'd taken this gesture for kindness, when all along, he'd been trading sympathy for information for his book. She pulled away from his arm and sat up. "I don't want to talk about chess," she said coldly.

Though he'd been caught prying, he didn't have the grace to look ashamed. "No, I guess you wouldn't," he said, his voice very dry. "Sorry. I thought you could use a little distraction."

"Thanks, anyway." Coffee rose, not knowing where she meant to go, but determined to put some space between them. Then she snapped to attention as the doctor walked into the room.

"Catherine Dugan?"

"Yes! Is she all right? Can I see her?" Coffee crossed the room in a few strides, then had to clasp her hands to keep from grabbing his lapels.

The doctor smiled. "Yes, she's badly bumped about, but we think she'll be fine. And I hope you will come talk to her—right away. We want to keep her overnight and she doesn't like the idea much."

That was putting it mildly. "No," Maureen said when Coffee had followed the doctor to the examination room. The older woman pursed her lips and started to cross her arms, then winced and abandoned the gesture. Her right wrist, which had been fractured, was now enclosed in a plastic brace and bandages. "I'm not staying here a minute more than I have to."

The doctor looked harassed, but his voice kept its sooth-
ing tone. "Now, Mrs. Dugan, we always have to consider
the possibility of concussion. We'd *really* like to keep you
for observation overnight."

Coffee stroked Maureen's good hand. "Maureen, if the
doctor really thinks—"

But Maureen shook her head vigorously, then looked over
Coffee's shoulder. "Dodge! You brought me here, didn't
you?"

Coffee turned to find Dodge lounging in the doorway, a
faint smile on his tanned face. "I did," he acknowledged.

"Well, then you can just take me home again! I've
banged up my knee and my wrist, but there's nothing wrong
with my head. I want out of here. I hate hospitals."

Dodge's eyes switched from Maureen's flushed face to
Coffee's, then back again. His shoulders lifted in the faintest
of shrugs. "All right," he said calmly. "When do you want
to go?"

"Now!" Maureen stated over a rising chorus of protest
from Coffee and the doctor. "Now will somebody please
bring me my clothes?"

"What did you do that for?" Coffee demanded when an
exasperated doctor had shooed her and Dodge out of the
room.

Dodge blew a little breath of annoyance. "You said you
admired her independence, Coffee? Then have the courtesy
to let her make her own decisions. She's certainly old
enough."

"But if anything's wrong with her—"

"She wants to take that chance." He set a hand lightly on
her shoulder. "And you'll be nearby, won't you?"

Coffee backed off a step, and his hand dropped away.
"Of course I will. But if there's some crisis in the middle of
the night . . ."

"I'll stay overnight on a couch, if you're worried," Dodge offered. "That way if there's any emergency. . ."

"Thanks, but I think you've caused quite enough trouble already, Dodge." Coffee turned on her heel and left him.

The trip home was a silent one. Sitting in front beside Dodge, Maureen seemed to have her attention turned inward. She was clearly hurting—the doctor had refused to give her any truly potent painkiller for fear it could mask the signs of concussion. Besides her bruised forehead and her fractured wrist, she had suffered a severely wrenched knee, which looked swollen to mountainous proportions under its ice pack.

The other occupants of the car were hardly more talkative. Though Dodge cast an occasional solicitous glance at Coffee's mother-in-law, he had withdrawn from Coffee entirely. Once, when his eyes met hers in the rearview mirror, it was as if he was glancing at a stranger.

Brooding alone in the backseat, Coffee was careful not to look in the mirror again. But all the same, Dodge Phillips ruled her thoughts. Why had he sided with Maureen? Was it for the reason he had given, which was praiseworthy enough, even though she thought it reckless and wrong?

Or had he sided with Maureen for a more devious reason? Could this be his way of broadening his bridgehead at the Owl Brook Inn? Because though Maureen had liked him before, now she looked on him as an ally. And Coffee thought she could anticipate his next move. With Maureen laid up for weeks, Dodge could always use her confinement as his excuse to come calling. There would be no way Coffee could turn him away.

He's outflanked me again, she thought and chewed her lip in frustration. It was not that she begrudged Maureen her visitors, but that she could see no way to keep Dodge and

Jeffie apart. *But I have to,* she thought, and hugged herself hard to contain a shiver. *I simply have to.*

As the car turned into the parking lot, she stirred, then glanced at her watch. Poor Anke had been holding the fort for several hours.

In the rush to get Maureen to hospital, there had been no time to summon outside aid. So Coffee had left Anke in charge of the house and, more importantly, of Jeffie. The young woman had been blaming herself bitterly for Maureen's accident—she'd seemed absolutely grateful for the chance to help in some way. Coffee only hoped that Anke had remembered to explain to the guests why no one had served them their traditional afternoon tea. She grimaced. There were sure to be complaints about that, whether Anke had explained or not. Well, that was the least of her worries.

The car stopped and she leaned forward just as Dodge turned around. This put them too close, nearly nose to nose, but Coffee clenched her fingers on his seatback and held her ground. "I'll make the daybed and clear the way, if you can wait a few minutes?" Maureen would not care for an audience when Dodge carried her in, if Coffee knew her own mother-in-law.

In the dim light, Dodge seemed to be looking at her lips rather than her eyes, though she couldn't be sure. He nodded and turned away.

When Coffee entered the Owl Brook, Mrs. Higby, a repeat guest of the bed and breakfast, was just leaving the guest lounge. "Oh, Coffee, there you are!" She patted her arm. "That new cook of yours is absolutely *marvelous!* Do you think you could persuade her to part with the recipe for those shortbread cookies she served at tea? They were to die for!"

"I'll, umm, ask her," Coffee promised, then stared at the woman's back as she headed upstairs. Anke had served the tea?

A heavenly aroma wafting from the back of the house seemed to confirm that conclusion. Coffee followed her nose to the kitchen.

Across the room, Jeffie knelt by a tower of wooden blocks. With one hand he was pointing sternly at Brigitta, who sat facing him on the far side of the tower. The toddler was almost levitating in her eagerness to join the game. "Not yet, Gitta," he commanded. With the other hand, Jeffie balanced a final block on the top row of his construction. "Okay, now!" he cried, and backed off.

With a squeak of delight, the little girl launched herself off the floor and went for the tower. Throwing her fat little arms wide, she hugged the building. Blocks clattered and flew. Shielding his face with his arms, Jeffie giggled as loudly as the little girl.

Across the room, Anke looked up from her work at the kitchen table and smiled. Then, catching a glimpse of Coffee, she wheeled around, her smile fading. She was wearing one of Maureen's flowered aprons, and she'd pulled her fine golden hair back in a knot, from which it was escaping in wispy tendrils. A smear of flour decorated one cheek. "She is well?" she asked eagerly, hurrying to meet Coffee. "Please, tell me she is well?"

"She is," Coffee assured her. The young woman looked so concerned, Coffee wanted to hug her. Instead, she touched her arm, then knelt as Jeffie ran toward her. She hugged him instead. "Hiya, big boy!"

"Mommy, where's Gram? Is she sick?" Luckily, Jeffie had been occupied upstairs and so had missed Maureen's accident entirely. Anke must have given him some sort of explanation.

"Gram's just fine," Coffee said, and squeezed him again. "She tripped on the stairs and hurt her arm and her knee, that's all." She looked up to smile at the hovering Anke. "That's all," she repeated firmly for her sake.

The woman let out a heartfelt sigh. "God be thanked!"

"Yes. And now I have to make the daybed. She's out in the car."

It took twice as long to make up the daybed in the family room with Jeffie and Anke trying to help her, and Brigitta gleefully joining in the activities, but Coffee was happy to put up with the fuss. Anke was almost singing with relief as she hurried to adjust a side table, find a vase of flowers to brighten it, then run back to the kitchen to put on a kettle for tea.

As she returned, Coffee stopped her. "Anke, Maureen will need peace and quiet. We can't let the children disturb her."

"Oh, no. But of course not!"

"I'm going to go tell Dodge to bring her in now. If any guests try to leave the lounge, do you think you could head them off for a minute, until we get her past that door?"

"Head them off?"

"Distract them. Talk to them."

Anke nodded, then, unexpectedly, a dimple appeared in her rounded cheek. "I shall ask them which is their favorite ski trail. That is all that they talk of anyhow, skiing."

"That will do it," Coffee agreed with an answering smile. Jeffie was standing beside her. She spread her hand flat on his soft hair. "You, big boy. Do you think you could keep Gitta busy in the kitchen until we get Gram settled? Then you can come have a teeny tiny visit, okay?"

Jeffie nodded. "We'll build another tower. Gitta loves 'em."

The transfer of Maureen from car to the family room went smoothly. Maureen looked frail but haughtily regal in Dodge's arms, as if she were accustomed to having handsome men carry her everywhere. But behind the fierce dignity, Coffee could see her exhaustion and pain. Indignation at Dodge stirred within her again, as the grand master deposited Maureen with exquisite care on the daybed. Maureen should have been in hospital—would have been, but for Dodge's interference.

He straightened, and their eyes met and locked. As if he could read her thought, his mouth twisted in a faint, lopsided smile. And though he didn't shrug, he might as well have.

But Coffee was the first to look away. She busied herself adjusting the pillows to prop up and protect Maureen's injured knee. "There now...would you like some more aspirin, Maureen?"

The older woman opened her eyes. "Please. And where are the children?"

"In the kitchen. Could you handle a very short visit from Jeffie? He's worried about you."

"Of course. And Gitta, too."

Coffee suppressed a smile. Anke had better watch out. Maureen was going to end up feeling as if she had a claim on the child, after trying to rescue her on the stairs. "All right." She stood, then turned to find Anke already waiting in the doorway, Gitta riding her hip and Jeffie standing at her side, his eyes wide with concern. "Come in," she called softly.

While Anke and Jeffie talked with Maureen in hushed, anxious voices, Coffee looked around for Dodge. She found him standing in the corner beyond the hearth, leafing through a red scrapbook. The hair stirred at the nape of Coffee's neck. She knew that scrapbook. It was one of the ones Maureen had maintained so lovingly while Richard was alive. Coffee had put them away in the attic three years ago.

She felt herself drawn across the room as if she were leashed by a noose of fine wire. "Just what do you think you're doing?" she asked in a furious undertone.

"What's it look like?" he said calmly, his voice equally low. "I told you this afternoon that Maureen meant to loan me this. Would you like me to ask her again?"

Coffee darted a look at Maureen's visitors. Jeffie's back was turned to them. He'd had eyes only for Maureen when he entered the room, but any second now, that could change. "No, take it and go."

"I thought you'd see it that way." Dodge closed the book with a snap and tucked it under his arm. "See me out?"

He knew the way, and she started to tell him so, then closed her mouth again. However she felt about the man personally, she couldn't deny that he'd been a great help. With a short nod she followed him into the hall, then along it to the front desk.

"You're sure you don't want me to stick around tonight?" Dodge's eyes seemed to be asking more than that simple question.

Coffee crossed her arms, barring herself from the pressure that, more and more, those dark, ironic eyes seemed to exert upon her. "No, thank you."

"I'm offering for Maureen, not for you, Coffee." His voice was very wry.

She felt her arms tighten and her cheeks warm, which was ridiculous, since he'd clearly not meant that as an innuendo. Then her cheeks grew even hotter, as his eyes flicked down to her breasts, framed and emphasized by that movement of her forearms. "I know that," she muttered, dropping her arms just as he smiled and turned away.

He scribbled a number on a notepad on the desk, ripped it off and swung back to hand it to her. "Here's my phone number, in case you change your mind. Call me anytime you need me, will you?"

"Yes. Okay." And now she had to get him out of there, had to make him stop looking at her like that. She had no defenses at all against his eyes, it seemed. Crossing to the door, she opened it for him.

His beautifully shaped mouth twisted as he passed by her. Clearly he felt himself thrown out.

She couldn't bear that. Not after the tenderness he'd shown Maureen today. "Dodge?" she said as he opened the storm door.

He turned back, his profile sharp and strong against the porch light.

"Thanks..." she continued. "I know you mean well."

Slowly he smiled. "Do I?" There was a clear note of mockery in his husky voice. A blast of cold air swept in to chill her, then he was gone.

What had he meant by that? Slowly, Coffee closed the inner door, then stood leaning back against it. The glass's chill penetrated her shirt and she shivered, crossed her arms, then hastily uncrossed them. Damn the man! How could he make her so self-conscious with just one look?

She started as, down the hall, Jeffie stepped out of the family room. Coffee let out a little sigh of thankfulness. At least that had gone well. Jeffie hadn't even noticed Dodge. With a smile, she came to meet him. "Okay, Jeffums?"

He nodded solemnly. "Gram's going to nap now. And Anke says to tell you your supper is ready. Me and Gitta ate hours ago."

"That sounds great. Want to sit with me while I eat mine?" They turned back down the corridor toward the kitchen, her hand riding his warm, narrow shoulder. "You run tell Anke I'm coming, and I'll go peek in on Gram, okay?"

Anke had made herself a great deal more than useful. Besides the beef stew for their supper, she'd made a wonderful broth from beef bones, shallots and wine for Maureen. She'd baked shortbread for the tea, and apparently she'd been mixing and kneading bread dough as if her life depended on it. The freezer was now crammed with frozen loaves braided and twisted into half a dozen enticing patterns. And to top it all off, she hadn't even made a mess of the kitchen. Coffee shook her head dazedly as she shut the freezer door. "You've been very busy," she said inadequately.

"When I worry, then I cook," Anke explained with a little smile as she brought a bowl of stew to the table for Coffee.

"Well, you needn't worry," Coffee told her. "What happened today was just an accident. It was nobody's fault. And Maureen is going to be fine."

"Yes, God be thanked. And now I go to sit with her, while you eat."

"I think she's dozing. Sleeping," Coffee added, when Anke looked blank.

Her face brightened. "That is good. And so I will sit in the dark." She slipped out of the room.

If it made her feel better, then she might as well, Coffee concluded with a little smile. She glanced across the kitchen to where Jeffie and Gitta were lying on their stomachs, pushing a choo-choo train of blocks back and forth across the linoleum between them. She let out a satisfied sigh. Thank heavens that those two had somehow made their peace today. Her lashes came down in a long, fluttering blink, then she shook her head and straightened up. She was exhausted, she realized suddenly.

Determinedly, Coffee set herself to finish the stew. She would send Jeffie up to bed early tonight, more for her own sake than for his. Tomorrow was going to be a long, hard day at Owl Brook Inn without Maureen's help. She would have to think about hiring someone to help her through the next month or two.

Her eyes returned to the children across the room. Gitta's golden head was pillowed on her fat little arms now. She'd had enough for the day, too. Coffee frowned. It went without saying that Anke and her daughter would stay the night. So she'd have to find some tactful way to waive their bill. She brightened. Of course—the baking more than paid for their room. She needn't manufacture a salve to Anke's pride at all. That would do. Tiredly, Coffee stood up from the table and beckoned, finger to her lips.

"Bedtime," she whispered to Jeffie. "I'll be sleeping down here with Gram tonight. But I'll come up in a few minutes to tuck you in."

But when Coffee stepped into Jeffie's room a short while later, all her hard won peace flew out the window.

Dressed in his teddy bear pajamas, Jeffie sat cross-legged on the quilt on his bed. It was a design that Maureen had made for him, with a central medallion of rose and sky blue squares. On the quilt squares, two double lines of coins faced each other in a familiar pattern. As Coffee stopped short, her fist rising to her breast, Jeffie reached to move a penny one square toward the opposing ranks. He was playing chess.

As she crossed the room, Coffee felt as if she were wading through ice water. Jeffie didn't look up when her shadow fell across his makeshift chessboard and she stopped beside him.

Oh, yes, she'd seen such concentration before. Richard had shut out most of life with that same laser beam of obsession. Her palms were so wet, she rubbed them against her thighs. "Jeffums..." she said hoarsely.

He didn't hear her. He picked up a coin from the opposite side of the board and brought it one square forward.

This was all Dodge's fault! She felt the hot flick of outrage beneath her ribs, then fought it down again. That was for later, but for now... She put a damp hand to Jeffie's soft hair, and he jerked his head with the same annoyed little twist that Richard had used so often. As if he were dodging a fly.

But she wasn't going to be brushed off this time. She should have fought harder for Richard. She'd fight as hard as need be for her son. *I will, Dodge,* she promised the distant man. *You bet I will.* She put her hand on Jeffie's shoulder and shook him gently. "Bedtime, young man."

This time he looked up at her, but his eyes were wide and unfocused.

"Bedtime," Coffee repeated, her heart sinking. She reached to take the coin he held from his fingers.

For a second he resisted, then he let it go. His luxurious lashes swept down, then up again, and suddenly he was with her. "Mommy."

"Bedtime," she repeated. "Let's put the money away, Jeffums."

"Money?" He looked down at the coins. "Oh. I'm playing chess. The game I played with Dodge."

The blood was pounding in her ears so loudly, it seemed to drown out his voice. Richard had been able to hold every move of dozens, perhaps hundreds of games in his head. But Jeffie... *Oh, please, not Jeffie.*

"I know where to move the king now. I made a mistake last time," Jeffie confided. "I won't make it again."

And neither would she, Coffee vowed, as she picked up Jeffie's emptied piggybank from off his desk and brought it over to the bed. Neither would she, if only she could figure exactly where she had gone wrong, or how to put it right again. All she knew was that in the midst of all her troubles stood the image of a dark, broad-shouldered man, like a black king—the still center around which the battle whirled.

CHAPTER SIX

ONLY ONE COUPLE LINGERED over their breakfast. It was snowing outside this morning, a gentle, fluffy snow that had enchanted the guests. Most were out playing in it already, and Coffee could hear others tramping downstairs, their footsteps heavy in their ski boots.

She finished clearing one of the tables, then stopped at the occupied table. "Well, what do you think? Would you like another pot of coffee?" she asked Mr. Grierson with a smile that belied her inner worries.

"Thanks, no—any more and we'll float away." He dabbed at his mouth with a napkin. "But...ah...we wouldn't mind a bit more of that coffee cake, if you've got any left, Coffee. That's the best darned stuff I've ever tasted. My compliments to the chef."

"I'll tell her. And yes, we've plenty more." Coffee bumped her way hip first through the back swinging door, then into the kitchen. She set down her tray on the counter, then smiled at Anke. "That makes it unanimous, Anke. Every one of our guests adores your coffee cake."

"So they should," Anke agreed, as she stacked dirty dishes into the washer. "It is the recipe of my mother. She cooked like an angel."

"And so do you." Coffee cut more wedges of the rich cake, picked up her tray and hurried back to the lounge. There were three more tables to clear, and by then she hoped the Griersons would be gone and she could start vacuuming. No, first she would check on Maureen and the children.

She paused for a moment by the far table, her eyes on the fluffy, drifting flakes beyond the window. Jeffie... She'd had nightmares about him last night. Some time after midnight she'd awakened with a protesting cry that had roused Maureen as well. She hadn't been able to remember the dream, only the menace of it—dark, tall shapes looming over Jeffie, calling him. After she'd given Maureen another dose of aspirin, she'd tiptoed upstairs to check on her son, even though she'd known he would be all right.

And I mean to keep him that way, she thought, her hands clenching the tray. Sometime today she would have to take that quilt from Jeffie's room. She'd tell him it needed dry cleaning. But would that even help? Now that she thought to look, the world seemed to be covered with checkerboards. Why, even the linoleum in the bathrooms was in black-and-white squares. Jeffie could find fuel for his obsession wherever he looked.

Her hands started moving again. She gathered the silverware, found room for the coffee cups and saucers. At least Maureen's misfortune had one bright side to it. Coffee now had an excuse to keep Jeffie nearby, rather than let him out to play with his friends as he normally would on a weekend. She'd asked him this morning to keep his grandmother company and to be ready to run errands if she needed anything. He'd also been assigned to ride herd over Gitta, who'd been consigned to the family room as well during the breakfast rush.

Pushing back into the kitchen, she found Anke polishing the top of the stove. Coffee smiled to herself. The woman was incredible. She'd been up an hour before Coffee, setting the guest tables and starting the coffee, and she hadn't shown any signs of slowing. "Anke, let's take a break," she called. "It's our turn to eat." Coffee brought the last pot of coffee over to the table, then collected the pan of cake from the oven.

But Anke was apparently more at ease while in motion. She perched on the edge of her chair across from Coffee, and broke her slice of moist, sweet cake into crumbling squares with her fork. She gulped her coffee so quickly that Coffee wondered that she'd didn't burn her mouth.

Her nervousness was contagious. After Coffee's first attempts at conversation were rebuffed with a startled smile and a shy monosyllable, she gave up and devoted her attention to the excellent pastry. Still, each time Coffee looked up, she found the German's wide blue eyes fixed on her face. And each time she caught Anke in this inspection, the girl's eyes darted away to a far corner of the kitchen. Coffee was almost relieved when the meal was over. "Well," she said as she folded her napkin. "We've finished the hard part, Anke. Everyone should be out skiing, so I can get to their rooms as I'm able. And most of them will be gone by tonight, so then it will get easier. But you've really been a wonderful help."

The blonde stared at her wide-eyed, not helping the conversation limp along in any way.

"So what about you?" Coffee asked. "When do you mean to leave?"

Anke clenched her hands on her cloth napkin. "I cannot."

"You can't?" Coffee repeated in confusion. She was too tired for guessing games this morning. "What do you mean? Is it your car, or—" Money. Was she entirely out of money?

"I cannot leave Maureen like this," Anke said, her voice vibrating with emotion. "I am to blame for her fall. So then—I cannot leave until she is well. I owe her this—this and so much more."

"Anke..." Coffee shook her head helplessly. "Good heavens, you're not to blame!"

"It was my baby on the stairs," Anke said stubbornly. "I *am* to blame. And so now I pay what I owe. To you, too." She'd been looking into the distance, somewhere over Coffee's shoulder. Now her blue eyes swung to stare into Coffee's with a passionate conviction. "You need my help, too, Coffee. This house is very big."

"Well, you've got that right." Slowly Coffee relaxed. Maybe the idea wasn't quite as crazy as it seemed at first thought. She had fully intended to hire someone to help out. And reliable help was hard to come by, in the height of tourist season. No one she could find would be half as capable or reliable as Anke—she was already convinced of that. "Have you discussed this with Maureen?" she asked, remembering the way the two women had had their heads together earlier this morning after Anke had brought Maureen her breakfast.

"Yes..." Anke twisted her napkin and her eyes darted away again.

"And what did she think?" Coffee prodded.

"She thought that she must think upon it."

"That sounds like a good plan," Coffee said with relief. "Let me see if she's considered the idea yet, and then we'll talk some more." When Coffee left the kitchen a minute later, Anke was scrubbing out the stainless-steel sinks as if her one chance at salvation depended on their spotlessness.

In the family room, Coffee found a tableau that stopped her in the doorway, a smile on her face. Maureen was propped up on her pillows, a blond child tucked under either arm. The three of them were absorbed in a cartoon show. Maureen looked sheepish as Coffee sank down on the chair beside them. "I haven't watched one of these in years," she confided in a voice low enough not to disturb her companions. Not that a bomb dropping down the chimney would have got their attention at the moment.

"You're sure you should let them up there?" Coffee worried.

"Oh, they're wiggle worms, but that's all right." Maureen smiled down at Gitta, who was scowling at the screen, her pink rosebud mouth contorted into a comic imitation of the cartoon villain's sneer.

"Okay." Maureen certainly looked happy enough. Coffee went on to describe in an undertone her conversation with Anke. "So what do you think?" she asked finally.

"I was going to ask you that," Maureen countered.

It was up to her? Coffee bit her lip thoughtfully. Anke was a darling, but there was this awkwardness between them that Coffee couldn't fathom. Shyness, she supposed. On the other hand, perhaps it was all in Coffee's head. Maureen certainly seemed to hit it off with the German. And clearly, she adored Anke's child.

She's never had a little girl to play with before, Coffee realized suddenly. Richard had been an only child, and Maureen had lost custody of him at an early age. Then she'd had Jeffie to lavish affection upon, but perhaps Maureen had always wanted a daughter or granddaughter to pamper? Coffee rubbed a fingertip along the toddler's velvety arm. Well, if that was so, who was she to stand in the way? She and Anke got on well enough, and no doubt they'd grow more comfortable as they worked together. "I think it sounds like a great idea," she said, and was rewarded with Maureen's beaming smile.

"Well . . ." Coffee leaned over Maureen to tickle Jeffie's nose. He gave her an absent sniff and went back to his program. "Guess I'll go tell Anke."

It was much later in the afternoon, after the guest rooms had been freshened, that Coffee sensed something was wrong. Carrying a basketful of dirty laundry, she'd stopped in on her way to the kitchen to see how Maureen was doing. Her mother-in-law was sleeping, and on the nearby couch, Gitta was also snuggled into a quilt and napping sweetly. There was no sign of Jeffie.

She hurried on to the kitchen, where Anke was starting the preparations for tea. "Anke, have you seen Jeffie?" she asked, careful to keep the worry from her voice.

Anke turned from the counter. "He is not in that room?"

"The sunroom?" Coffee opened the intervening door and stepped down into the area. No one was there.

"A little time ago, he passed this way," Anke said behind her.

Let him be up in his room, Coffee thought desperately, as she nodded and walked to the steps that led down to the mudroom. Propped against the wall below, she could see her own skis, but not her son's. Her heartbeat stampeded. *He might be anywhere,* she told herself. But if Jeffie had wanted to visit one of his little friends, he knew the rules. He would have asked permission. And since he had not...

Coffee spun around. "Anke, it looks like it's going to be a very small tea. The Higbys just left, and most of the rest are still out skiing. Do you think you might handle it by yourself? I'll try to come back in time, but—"

"Please do not worry. It is no problem," Anke assured her.

In spite of her worries, Coffee had to smile as she slipped into her ski jacket and boots and hurried out the mudroom door. Anke had gotten the Americanism half-right, anyway. She sobered again as she stepped into her ski bindings and slipped the ski-pole thongs over her fingers. Half-obliterated by the falling snow, a ski track led from the back door in a purposeful slash down the hill. Toward the trail that led to Dodge's cabin.

But she'd taken only a stride in pursuit when she heard the growl of a car turning into the front parking lot. Coffee slid to a halt and stared over her shoulder. They weren't expecting more guests tonight, but walk-ins weren't unheard of. And Anke had not yet learned check-in procedures, or anything about room rates. With a hiss of frustration, Coffee poled along the snow-covered flat of the side driveway toward the front of the house.

As she rounded the corner, Dodge's black Porsche backed into a parking space. A door swung open and Jeffie tumbled into view, his face alight with excitement. The other door opened, and Dodge Phillips swung out at a more leisurely pace. He met Jeffie at the back of the car and lifted Jeffie's skis off the ski rack. "Here you go, buddy." He handed them to the child. Then his chin came up as he spotted Coffee over her son's shoulder.

Would she ever be able to approach this man without her heart trying to kick its way out of her ribcage? Coffee took a steadying breath, then turned to her son. "Jeffie, I thought you were taking care of Gitta for us?"

Jeffie's cheeks were already flushed with the cold, and now they deepened a shade. "She's asleep. And I'm tired of playing with babies." His worshipful glance up at Dodge showed clearly who he'd rather be playing with. "We drove home the long way. Dodge said we could."

Dodge let out a little groan that turned into a fit of coughing as Jeffie smiled up at him proudly and Coffee glared daggers.

She jabbed a pole into the snow on each side of her skis. "Well, she's going to wake up any time now, if I know Gitta," she said. "And meantime, Anke could use some help serving tea. So scoot, young man."

Jeffie departed reluctantly but resolutely, like a very short soldier marching off to war, his skis slanted over one shoulder. But the moment Coffee turned to blast Dodge, Jeffie swung back and called, "Hey, Dodge?"

Dodge's wary expression relaxed into a smile. "Yeah?"

"Thanks for the ride!" Jeffie wheeled again and started up the stairs.

Coffee blinked. It had been an oddly man-to-man exchange. Her baby was growing up. And she wanted him to keep on growing, but straight and tall, not blighted by the obsessive winds that this man had brought with him. Her brows drew together again as she turned back to Dodge.

"Hey, Dodge?" Jeffie called from the porch behind her. This time he sounded all little boy. "You coming in?"

"Maybe." Dodge waved him inside with a casual flip of the hand, like a catcher lofting a soft one to a teammate at the end of an inning, then swung back to Coffee, the laughter still sparkling in his eyes. "Persistent, isn't he?"

That made two of them. But with all the interruptions, Coffee was losing the thread of her tirade. She lost it entirely as the storm door opened, and Jeffie and two of her guests tramped down the front steps.

"My cap," Jeffie said, "'s in the car. The Porsche," he added proudly.

"Door's unlocked." Dodge chuckled and caught Coffee's elbow. "Want to come show me the river, Coffee?" He waited for her to step out of her skis, then pulled her across the parking lot toward the road. "You can yell at me in peace down there," he explained under his breath.

It wasn't a bad idea, though she felt as if she were being deflated by an expert. She looked back over her shoulder and saw that Jeffie was drifting along behind them, his eyes wide with interest.

Dodge had glanced back, too. "Hey, bud—inside," he called. "You've got a job to do."

Jeffie turned around and went. Coffee felt her blood pressure rise a notch. What did it take to win such unquestioning obedience—a set of baritone vocal cords and a five o'clock shadow?

Dodge led her to the middle of the little bridge over Owl Brook and dropped her arm. Brushing the cap of snow off the iron railing, he rested his forearms on the parapet and leaned over to stare down at the brook. Automatically, she came to lean beside him. Thirty feet below, the water roared under its fresh mantle of white. Here and there where the current ran fiercest, she could see the black, rolling water itself. The planks of the bridge rumbled as her guests drove their car across. They beeped their horn merrily and sped off toward the valley.

Dodge leaned over and brought his lips almost to her ear. "It wasn't really the long way home," he said. "It was the quickie excursion, up by Black Mountain and back again."

She turned toward him partly to glare at him, partly to remove her ear from the warm caress of his breath.

He gave her a rueful grin. "I guess I was showing off," he conceded. "It's not often I find somebody who likes my toys as much as I do."

That boyish grin of his pulled her the way the river sucked along a tumbling pine branch. She caught the edge of the railing to steady herself. "I told you to stay away from Jeffie."

"You did," Dodge agreed. "But how am I supposed to stay away from the kid, when he comes and flattens his nose on my plate-glass window? There I was, minding my own business, playing chess with my computer, and next thing I know—"

"You *didn't* let him watch you play!" Coffee exploded. "Dodge, you know how I feel—"

He put a black-gloved hand over her nearest mitten. "Yes, you've made that very plain," he said wryly. "So I figured the best thing to do was hustle him out of there and take him back to you. And that's all I did."

"That's *not* all you did!" Suddenly she was close to tears. "He was playing chess by himself last night—using his quilt for a chessboard."

"Was he!" Dodge tried to hide his look of pleasure and failed miserably. "Coffee, you can't stop this. You're crazy to even try."

"Who do you think you are?" she said between her teeth. "You walk in here out of nowhere, and you think you know what's best for my son?"

"I think I do," he said calmly. "I've been there, where he is now—though I don't pretend that I showed the same grasp at his age. But, yes, I know what it's like to ride the tiger of your own talent...."

He hung on to her hand when she would have drawn it away. "Coffee, you've got to understand this," he said eagerly. "The kind of genius Jeffie's got—he's *got* to ride it, or it'll ride him. He's got to learn to control it. And I could show him how."

"We don't need your help! We were doing fine without it!"

"Were you?" His tone had shifted; the question taunted even as it caressed her. "Were you really, Coffee?" His fingers tightened on hers.

They might have been squeezing her heart, or feathering softly, deliberately down her spine. She shuddered and whipped her head around to stare back toward the inn. The timer that controlled the electric candles in all the windows had switched on. The house glowed like an illustration in an old-fashioned Christmas card. If she hadn't been doing fine this past three years, at least that—the Owl Brook Inn—was what she'd been doing. And she *had* been happy, until this man came along. She had to remember that. She'd be happy again, when he was gone. But somehow, with his thumb smoothing her fingers, it didn't feel that way.

Doggedly, she forced her thoughts away from her own loneliness and back to the problem at hand. "Do you mean to mention Jeffie in your book?" she asked dully. She swung back to face him.

"Yes," Dodge replied. "He's fascinating. Chess genius almost never breeds true, Coffee. There are a lot of theories why. Some think it's an Oedipal conflict—that the father can't tolerate the chance of being dethroned by his son. So he stamps out the child's talent at an early age."

Remembering the fear in Richard's eyes the last time he'd played Jeffie, she could almost believe that theory. How strange, that had he lived, Richard might have discouraged Jeffie from playing. But he hadn't lived to do that. And so she would have to. "You can't write about Jeffie," she said, and yanked her hand away from his.

"I can." He turned to lean on the railing again.

"No!" She caught his forearm, determined to make him see. "You can't. I won't let you. Didn't you ever look at Richard—really look at him? Didn't you look at that scrapbook Maureen loaned you? Did you ever see him smile? I won't let you do that to Jeffie, Dodge. I won't!" She looked down to find that she was pounding on his arm with clenched fist.

"Easy!" Swinging around, he caught her wrist, then hooked his other arm round her waist. "Take it easy, will you?" He gave her a little shake.

Suddenly the tears she'd been fighting overflowed. "Damn!" She choked and turned her head aside.

He brought her the rest of the way in against him and locked her there with the arm at her back. His chin came down lightly on the top of her head. "Hey, easy..." he said in an entirely different tone of voice.

She spread her free hand against his jacket to push him away, then somehow lost the impulse. She was wrapped in warmth and infinite strength.... She let out a shuddering little sigh and leaned against him.

"Easy..." he murmured and rubbed his cheek across her hair.

She could have stayed like this—being rocked ever so slightly back and forth in his arms, the river rushing below them, his heart pounding against hers, snowflakes falling on her lashes. She could have stayed this way forever, but headlights swept over them, then a car rumbled across the bridge only feet away. It was some of her guests—the car swung into the parking lot. Coffee tried to back away, but Dodge held her in place.

"Be still," he said crisply, "and let me think."

So she nodded and stood there, letting him think. But with the car's passing she'd lost the peace that she'd found for a moment. There would be knowing smiles to face back at the inn now. The thought of them made her suddenly conscious of the shape and hardness of his body, of the fact that her breasts were flattened against his chest. That in spite of the falling snow, she was as warm as—as— She dismissed the notion of an oven and twisted restlessly in his grasp. This time his arms eased to let her retreat half a step. His hands shifted to her arms.

"Then what about a trade?" he asked her. His black hair was spangled with snowflakes. A perfect one landed on his left eyebrow and he shook his head impatiently.

"A trade?" she asked warily.

"I want information. You want me to leave Jeffie out of this book. Seems to me we have grounds for a trade." He reached to brush a snowflake off her nose, then gave her a lopsided smile. "So how does this sound? I promise to leave Jeffie out of the biography entirely. You promise to come talk to me. Tell me about Richard."

She shook her head instantly. She'd never talked with anyone about Richard, and she didn't want to start now. Not with this man, of all people.

"No?" His smile was regretful—and utterly unyielding. "Well, it seemed like a good idea. Guess I'll have to stick with the original plan. Maureen seems pretty open to helping me."

And if he continued to interview Maureen, inevitably, he and Jeffie would come into contact. Coffee clenched her hands till they hurt.

And there was something else to consider. What if Maureen let something slip about Richard's suicide? It was she, after all, who had found the letter.

But surely Maureen would guard that fact, no matter how much she liked Dodge, Coffee argued with herself. Maureen had been raised Catholic, after all. The manner of Richard's death had to wound her as deeply as it did Coffee. She wouldn't want that to make it into print. But still . . . trusting Dodge as she did, Maureen might let something slip.

On the other hand . . . Coffee took a deep breath. If she herself became Dodge's prime source of material, then she could control the facts she fed him—make sure he never learned the truth. She raised her eyes to his, and felt the little jolt of electricity as their gazes locked.

His eyes were catching light from somewhere—either the snow itself or the lights of the inn. Warm candlelight or bits of ice, which was she seeing in those dark eyes? She'd have given a lot to know.

And who was she kidding, telling herself that she could control this man? He'd been one step—no, several steps ahead of her since the first time they'd met. A grand master, like Richard he would see five, six, seven moves ahead of where he was playing at any point in a chess game. And in life? she wondered. Was that what he was doing? Stalking and herding her toward a conclusion that only he could yet see?

"Well?" he murmured.

Did she really have a choice? And wasn't that what chess was all about—the ruthless and systematic removal of your opponent's choices until he was driven to the final square of his defeat?

But I'm not there yet, she thought, and took a deep breath. They were barely into the middle game, as Richard would have said.

And Richard would also have said that the hungriest player, rather than the most talented, usually won. Well, Dodge Phillips couldn't hunger for victory in this game half as much as she did, with her son to protect.

She lifted her chin and looked him straight in the eye. "Okay," she said softly. "You've got yourself a deal."

CHAPTER SEVEN

"YOU'RE LOOKING FANCY," a cheerful voice observed in Coffee's ear.

Jumping half a foot, she dropped the skillet she'd been washing, then spun around from the kitchen sink.

Peter Bradford stood before her, a puzzled grin on his face and a large bunch of daisies clutched in one hand. "Sorry!" the ski patrolman added. "Didn't mean to scare you like that. I knocked, but you didn't hear me."

"That's okay, Peter." Coffee gave a rueful laugh. "Guess I'm just jumpy tonight." Jumpy was an understatement. She was due down at Dodge Phillips's cabin in half an hour. She studied the blue wool shirtwaist dress she was wearing and grimaced. The effect she'd been striving for was one of cool formality, a visual message to reinforce the business-like tone she meant to set at their conference. But perhaps she should have stuck to shirt and jeans. She wouldn't want Dodge to think she thought this interview was something special. Placing the skillet in the drainer, she shut off the tap. "What are you up to with those flowers?"

"For Maureen. I heard she had an accident."

"You heard right," Coffee agreed as she dried her hands on a dish towel. "Hang on a minute and I'll take you to her." She set about adding soap to the dishwasher. They had finished supper only minutes before, eating on trays in the family room with Maureen. But Coffee had not been able to stomach a bite. She was not looking forward to this evening.

"You must have read my mind," Peter said, eyeing her dress. "I meant to ask if you wanted to go find some music, after I visit with Maureen."

Coffee smiled and shook her head. "'Fraid I have to go out, Peter." When he raised his brows, she considered explaining, then decided not to. Peter had no claim on her company, after all. He was just a friend—had been ever since high school. But she found Dodge Phillips too disturbing to discuss—even with a friend.

"Anything to do with that guy who's moved in down the hill?" Peter wondered shrewdly.

Coffee sighed. Small-town living had its drawbacks. If you sneezed up here on the hill, half of Jackson caught a cold. "He's invited me down for a drink." Commanded, was more like it. Last night on the bridge she'd tried to put him off for a day or two, but Dodge had cut through her excuses with a few incisive questions. He wanted to get moving on his book research. *And I suppose I want him to get moving, too,* Coffee reminded herself. The sooner he got what he wanted, the sooner he'd leave them all in peace. Still, she was not looking forward to this meeting.

"Well, watch out for them city slickers," Peter warned her, only half whimsically. "Anybody drives a Porsche ain't to be trusted." He snapped off a daisy, set the bunch down on the counter and caught the thick braid she'd pulled her hair into. "Now turn around."

Nose squinched in mock protest, she did so, and he tucked the blossom behind her ear. "There—outfit complete," Peter decided.

She gave him a wary smile, uncertain as to whether her "date" had just been given his blessing or if this was a subtle form of male branding. Peter had made it known that if

she ever wanted him as more than a friend, he was willing.
But for some reason she could never explain, she just
couldn't feel that way. "Thanks, friend," she said lightly.

His good-natured grimace said that the message had been
received. Then the kitchen door swung open and Gitta pat-
tered through with a giggling shriek.

From out in the corridor, a hollow, ghastly voice boomed.
"Gitta, where *are* yoouu? Gitta, I'm gonna *get* yoouu! Are
you in the *bath*room?" Jeffie's voice faded as he checked
out that room.

The little girl whirled around, looking for a hiding place,
then ran right at Peter. Grabbing his leg, she swung around
it to hide behind him. She buried her face against the back
of his leg, giggling half-hysterically.

Peter craned to look over his shoulder. "What's this?" he
laughed.

"*This* is Gitta. Her mother is working for us while Maureen's down."

"Where *are* you?" Jeffie groaned from the doorway.
"Here I *come!*"

The little girl shrieked, stamped her tiny feet in excitement and hugged Peter's leg all the harder, her face hidden
as if that would hide her from her pursuer.

"Hooo! *Haaah!*" Jeffie stomped with long, menacing
strides into the kitchen, saw Peter and stopped, discon-
certed.

But peeking around her shelter, Gitta spotted Jeffie. With
a shriek, she turned to flee along the counter and tumbled
over Coffee's feet. She landed with a thump in a perfect
belly flop, then let out a breathless bawl.

"Uh-oh!" Peter stooped along with Coffee, and brought
the crying child to her feet. "Bet that hurt, didn't it?"

Eyes squinched shut, Gitta sobbed her wholehearted
agreement.

A shamefaced Jeffie drifted over to join them. "Is she okay?"

"Sure, she is," Peter said easily. "Everything but her pride. A girl doesn't like to take a nosedive in front of an audience." Reaching up to the counter, he brought down his bouquet and snapped off another blossom. "Here, sugar." He twirled the daisy near the tip of her pink snub nose.

"Gitta, what is this?" Anke bustled into the kitchen just as Peter's attentions reduced the child's howls to a hiccuping sob.

Gitta grabbed the flower from his hand, examined it and scowled. Then, starting to sob even louder, she held the daisy and her arms out to her mother as Anke knelt beside the other adults.

"She took a tumble," Peter explained to Anke.

"Please?"

"She fell."

"Ah? Yes. She is a clumsy, clumsy girl." Anke buried her face in the side of the toddler's neck and made a playful, blowing sound. "Gitta...Brigitta..." She blew on the child again, and suddenly Gitta's sobs changed to a reluctant chortling. Peter watched, fascinated, and seeing his eyes widen, Coffee smiled to herself and picked up the flowers.

She passed them to the ski patrolman. "Better save a few of these for Maureen," she warned. At the moment, he looked as if he'd just as soon hand them over to a certain blonde.

Standing, Coffee checked her watch and her smile faded. "Anke, would you take Peter here to Maureen?" she asked the German. "I'm late." As she turned her back, Peter was shaking Anke's hand, his craggy face very serious. Anke looked just as solemn, but her dimple was showing.

Coffee put a hand on her son's shoulder. "No more chasing tonight, big boy," she told him. "Anke will want to put Gitta to bed soon. So you ought to let her settle down first. And you have homework to do."

Jeffie made a face, and she tweaked the end of his nose. "Why don't you bring your books down and do it with Gram and Peter?" she suggested. She would just as soon he didn't retreat to his room until he was ready for bed. She had changed his quilt for a wool blanket, but she had little doubt about her son's ingenuity. If he wanted a chessboard, he'd make one somehow. It was better to keep him otherwise occupied. Really, Gitta was proving to be as much a blessing as Anke.

"You're gonna go see Dodge, aren't you?" Jeffie demanded.

When he'd asked where she was going earlier, Coffee had simply given him a mischievous smile and told him that she was going "out." But she couldn't duck a direct question. "Yes," she said briefly. How did he know? Or was it just that Dodge was always on his mind?

"Can I come?"

"No, bugaboo. You have homework to do." Coffee kissed the corner of his scowl, then hurried down the connecting passage to the garage.

She was half an hour late by the time she reached Dodge's cabin. Biting her lip with vexation, she knocked on his front door, waited, then knocked again. Could he have gone out? But a plume of white smoke was rising from the chimney. She raised her hand to knock a third time and the door opened.

"There you are," Dodge said. Backlit by a warm golden light, he looked very tall and wide enough to fill the doorway. Coffee took half a step back, then stopped herself. It was too late to retreat now.

"I'd about given up on you," Dodge continued. He caught her arm and drew her into the house. "Come in before we let all the heat out."

He had heat enough to spare, Coffee thought ruefully as he helped her out of her coat. The weight of his hands on her shoulders seemed to bring the hot blood rushing to the surface of her skin. He must have overstoked his wood stove, she told herself. Novices tended to do that.

Leaving the coat in his hands, she walked on into the room. Except for a light over the sink in the kitchen, the room was lit only by the kerosene lamp on the counter that divided the space, and by the fire, roaring behind its glass door. She turned around nervously, looking for a safe place to sit.

"I was just doing the dishes," Dodge told her with a smile. The sleeves of his black wool shirt were rolled up to the elbows.

Her eyes skated over the swirling, dark hair on his forearms, then darted away.

"Come talk to me while I finish." He nodded toward the kitchen.

The little galley was too cramped for both of them, she thought, but was unable to voice the protest. She moved to lean against the refrigerator, but Dodge touched her arm and eased her on down the counter. "Let me get you a drink." He poured out a glass of white wine, handed it to her, then collected his own from where it waited near the sink.

He tapped her glass lightly with his own. "To..." His eyes skimmed over her face—down to her lips, then back up to her eyes.

Just your imagination, she thought edgily. She wanted to cross her arms, but couldn't while holding the glass of wine, and had to settle for clenching her free hand around the edge of the counter.

His eyes followed the gesture and lingered there. "To winter," he said, and sipped his wine.

Coffee took a quick swallow as well, set her glass down smartly and jumped at the noise it made.

Dodge set his own glass beside hers. "And to talkative women," he added, amusement shimmering behind his words. He picked up a plate and rubbed a sponge across it. "So how's Maureen?"

Gradually, under his offhand but thorough questioning, Coffee began to talk. He didn't really care how she'd spent her day, she told herself. This was simply his means of putting her at ease. And to some extent it was working. With most of his attention fixed on his dishes, she was freed from the disturbing power of his eyes. Leaning against the counter beside him, she was free to watch his long, competent hands. Free to study the way his mouth curled at the corners even when he wasn't smiling, as if he would find the world entertaining even at the darkest of times.

But her uneasiness returned as he shut the water off. "Come sit down," he said, and touched her shoulder. Shying away from his fingers, she moved ahead of him into the living room.

The easy chair that she would have chosen had a mountainous stack of books piled upon it. So did the chair that was drawn up to face a computer sitting on the desk in the corner. That left only the couch. Looking again at the chair, she shot a suspicious glance over her shoulder at Dodge. Had he again anticipated her move and blocked it? *Knight to queen's three,* she thought, nibbling her lip. He was kneeling by the fire, feeding more wood to the red-hot coals. Seen in profile, the curve at the corner of his mouth seemed to have deepened, but perhaps that was only the firelight.

He came to join her on the couch almost immediately, switching on a lamp, then reaching to pick up a book from the coffee table—Richard's scrapbook. "Well, shall we get started?"

So she had been wrong. He wasn't stalking her romantically—at least not at the moment. It should have been reassuring to realize that, but somehow wasn't. One worry simply replaced the other. She didn't want to think about Richard tonight. But Dodge lifted a notepad and pen off the table, then opened the scrapbook and spread it across both their laps. "Maureen's notations are pretty cryptic, and her handwriting's worse. Do you know what tournament this was?" He tapped a photo on the first page.

"Yes." She knew these pages by heart. Richard had loved to look at his own scrapbooks, and he'd given her blow-by-blow accounts of all his victories. "That was in Chicago, the first year he was playing."

Dodge's pen scratched on the paper. "He'd have been nine?"

"Eight..." Only a year older than Jeffie. She stared down at Richard's brooding face on the page, and felt her heart constrict. *No, not that for Jeffie.* If she had to endure Dodge's interviews from now to summer to keep Jeffie out of his book, out of that life, then she'd willingly pay the price. Pay it a hundred times over.

"And who is this player? Do you know him?"

As the minutes, then the hour passed, the pages of Dodge's notebook slowly filled with his angular, bold writing. He rose once to refill their glasses and once to stoke the fire again, but each time he returned, he maintained the same circumspect distance between her thigh and his on the couch. Gradually, as she became sure that he meant to make no move on her, Coffee relaxed. Perhaps it was the heat of the room, or the wine, or the soft, deep rasp of Dodge's methodical questions. She felt as if she were sinking into a red-gold haze of memory, that she was reciting by rote a story that had happened to someone else, somewhere else, far away and long ago.

As she spoke, Dodge's unswerving attention became almost a physical sensation. It seemed to press upon her skin with a lazy, hypnotic weight. Her nerves expanded and prickled as if someone were brushing her hair out before a fire. Her lashes fluttered once, and were heavier when she lifted them. The room was very warm....

Dodge turned the last page, then rested his hand upon it. "You two seem so different," he observed casually. "What attracted you to him?"

Her lashes drooped again as she tried to remember and recite the facts. "Oh...his intelligence... And he seemed to know just what he wanted... At eighteen, that's pretty rare...most kids are confused. They don't know who they are or what they want...."

"And he wanted you?" Dodge asked so quietly that his words merged with the murmur of the fire.

She smiled, a rueful, bittersweet smile, and slowly leaned back against the cushions. "He wanted me." He'd wanted her, she later realized, as Richard had always wanted victory. Her initial resistance had been like a red cape to a bull.

"And I suppose the only way he could get you was to marry you?"

Coffee opened her eyes. They weren't talking about photographs. How had they moved to this personal level? She swung around to find that Dodge had turned sideways and had propped an arm along the back of the couch behind her. Their faces were only inches apart. She drew back and found the armrest of the couch blocking further retreat. A tiny spark of panic lit within her, like the flare of a struck match.

"As a matter of fact, yes," she answered, her voice very cool and precise, even as she felt her cheeks warm. "I was a bit of a prude in those days." His unflinching gaze felt like a hot hand laid against her cheek. The blush deepened until her eyes watered, and she swung away from him. And now he was going to lean even closer and ask her if she was still a prude. And when he did, she was going to get up and go.

He didn't ask it. He asked something worse. "And what happened after he'd won?"

That was enough—more than enough! Gathering her feet under her, she shot him a furious look and started to rise. But his hand settled on her far shoulder. Unbalanced, she dropped back against the cushions. "I don't mean sexually," he cut in as she opened her mouth to protest. "I'm talking chess. Your husband never showed much interest in rematches. Once he knew he could beat an opponent, he looked for a tougher one. Did he stay interested in you, Coffee, once he'd won the game?"

She'd asked herself that a thousand times at least—what had happened to Richard's relentless, all-consuming passion once they had married? Where had it gone? Had she simply been a flesh-and-blood queen to be conquered, then swept from his board? Was that all? Or was it just that chess had swallowed up all of his time and energy after that, leaving nothing of him for her? She parted her lips to answer, then slowly shut them again. She didn't know. Wouldn't have answered this man's merciless probing had she known.

His hand seemed to rise through the haze of her introspection. The side of his warm, rough knuckle brushed along her bottom lip. "I would have," he said, his voice very low and almost harsh.

Would have? It took her a moment to think back to his question—long enough for his knuckle to stroke back across her mouth the other way. *I would have stayed interested in you, once I'd won,* he was saying? Proudly she lifted her chin and looked away.

Maybe, but Richard would have said exactly the same thing, while he was pursuing her. That and anything else he had to say to win her heart. And last time, it had worked. But she wasn't a girl of eighteen anymore, ready to believe that passionate words, or ruthless pursuit, equaled love.

Resting a forefinger against her chin, Dodge urged her head back around to face him. "Okay, here's an easier question," he said. He gave her a smile, but there was something strained about it. "After your marriage, did you stay interested in him?"

He was as brutal in his quest for facts as ever Richard had been in his quest for victory. But then, why should that surprise her? He was a chess grand master—Richard's brother under the skin. His finger feathered up the line of her jaw, traced the curve of it up to her hair, then outlined the rim of her small ear. She shivered, a liquid, rippling motion that came from deep within, then shook her head and kept on shaking it. No, she wasn't going to make the same mistake twice, no matter how much she might want— She shook her head again, shaking that thought aside, and rose.

He made no move to stop her. "That was a no? You didn't stay interested?" he asked with soft mockery.

"That was a no, I'm *not* interested!" she said, rounding on him fiercely. Who was he to come crashing into her life this way, making her feel this way, when— "I'm tired of game players." She stalked toward the front door. "I'm tired of games." Her head jerked in surprise as she realized he was padding along right on her heels.

"Ah . . ." he said softly. "That's one question I haven't asked yet."

"What's that?" she asked, yanking her coat off the coat rack.

Without answering, he took the coat from her hands and held it up for her. She stared at the garment as if it were a waiting trap. But she couldn't leave without it. With an impatient sigh that was meant to conceal her fear, she turned her back and slid her arms into its sleeves.

He brought the coat up over her shoulders. Then, still holding its lapels, he rested his fists against her collarbones, his arms encircling her, and rocked her gently back against the hard, warm length of him. His face brushed her hair and his fists pressed more firmly against her as she shuddered. "I haven't yet asked...what's wrong with games?" he murmured, his breath tickling her ear.

Trust him to feel that way! While she...she was another kind of person entirely. She couldn't play at love—never could. It would never be just a game to her. His left fist rested just above her heart, which she could feel pounding. No doubt Dodge could, too. And God help her, she wanted his hand to stay there, wanted his fingers to open and take her. Wanted his arms to slide down and around her, to hold her tightly and never let her go. With another rippling shudder, she pressed forward against his fists, until they eased their pressure, then fell away.

It was only two long, lonely strides to the door. She took them without looking back. "There's nothing wrong with games—for some people," she said, and walked out into the night. After the warmth of his arms, the cold air was like a bucket of ice water in the face. Bracing and raw...and utterly unwelcome.

CHAPTER EIGHT

To REACH JACKSON, it was necessary to turn off the highway that led north through the White Mountains and cross the old covered bridge that spanned the Ellis River. The bridge had been one of Coffee's favorite haunts since childhood. With time on her hands, she naturally gravitated there. Stepping out of her skis, she propped them against the first pair of X-crossed timbers that reinforced the half walls of the structure. She strolled out along the shadowy pedestrian walk, absently waving to old Mr. Hazard as his car rumbled across the wooden roadbed and passed her on its way into town. The grumble of the car's engine and the rush of the river below echoed off the tin roof overhead.

The age-darkened pine framework was scarred with the names of generations of Jackson kids. Coffee slowed her steps, then smiled as she came to the beam where she and Elsa Warner had carved their names that day they had played hookey from junior high. Like most of the carvers, they had ended their inscription with the date. But in their case, the last numeral was missing. It simply read 198—. The gouge in the wood that followed the eight was where Elsa's blade had slipped when she saw her mother's car approaching the bridge. Coffee laughed to herself and walked on. She would have to give Jeffie a knife for his next birthday—he was almost old enough.

Reaching the center of the bridge, she leaned on the railing to stare down at the river. Nearly an hour till Jeffie's school let out. She meant to meet him as she had done the day before, then ski up to the inn with him. That was the surest way to make certain he didn't stop by Dodge's cabin. Another car turned off the highway, then rumbled past, but she didn't turn to see who it was. A tourist, from the speed he was driving. The locals took life at a saner pace.

Not that her own life had felt all that sane recently. Coffee let out a little sigh. She hadn't had much sleep last night, after leaving Dodge. Her flannel nightgown—normally the coziest of garments—had seemed too rough, too warm, against her suddenly sensitive and overheated skin. And she'd awoken this morning to find that sometime in the night she'd slipped out of the gown entirely. With a little hiss of displeasure, she concentrated on the water below. The river was shallow and filled with snow-capped boulders. Gurgling and shouting, it dashed itself to foam and gleaming splinters as it fought its way south.

Coffee jumped violently as someone leaned on the railing beside her.

"I've been meaning to do this for days," Dodge Phillips said.

"You have?" *A witty retort,* she jeered at herself, and searched a mind gone blank for something else to say. But she'd made the mistake of meeting his eyes, and found that it took all her psychic energy simply to break their hold on her. And she could feel her heart beating, like a distant echo of the river below. Darn the man, how could he affect her so? Richard had never— She ducked that thought like a skier dodging an eye-level branch at trailside, then jerked around to stare down at the water. "Yeah, it's a nice place," she muttered, directing her words at the river.

"Must be wonderful when it rains," Dodge observed, tipping his head back to survey the rafters' rugged symmetry. "I'm a sucker for tin roofs."

So was she. She hunched her shoulders and clamped her hands together. *Oh, go away, Dodge. Please go away. You scare me.* Scariest of all was that she didn't want him to go, that somehow without looking, she knew to the quarter inch how far she would have to drift sideways to bring her arm into contact with his. She let out a shaky breath. This was ridiculous. It was just that she hadn't been touched in so long, the way he'd touched her last night. It had nothing to do with him. Any man's touch would have had the same affect on her. *Liar,* she told herself rudely.

Meantime he'd been talking. "—Since I'm headed up there now?" he finished on an inquiring note.

She had a fifty percent chance of being right, whatever she answered. "Yes," she mumbled to be agreeable.

"Good, then let's go." Dodge hooked his fingers under her elbow and started her toward the Jackson side of the bridge.

"Where?" She pulled away from him to grab her skis as they came to them, and he transferred his hand to the small of her back. Light as his touch was, she could feel it through two layers of sweaters.

He glanced at her in surprise. "To visit Maureen, I said. I've been down in North Conway, finding her a book and a nice, decadent-looking box of chocolates. She does like chocolates?"

"No." Coffee stopped short.

"She doesn't?" Dodge took the skis out of Coffee's hands. His dark eyes registered amusement rather than distress. "Then I guess I'll have to feed them to you, won't I?"

"I mean no, you can't come up to the house. Jeffie will be getting out of school in half an hour."

Dodge shrugged as he lifted her skis to the ski rack on his car, which was parked at the side of the road. "So?"

"So we made a deal, Dodge Phillips! You were going to leave Jeffie alone, if I agreed to talk to you."

"Wrong." Dodge opened the passenger seat for her and stood waiting, a look of impatience clouding his previous smile. "We agreed that I'd leave Jeffie out of my book, if you talked to me. And speaking of which, when can we have our next session?"

He was rushing her on purpose, not giving her time to get her teeth into one issue before he presented the next. It reminded her of speed chess, that lightning-fast version of the game that Richard had adored, where no clock was used and one move followed the next like the punch and counter-punch of two boxers. She shook her head in frustration, then gave up and got in the car. If he meant to see Maureen, he would see Maureen. So all she could do was expedite the visit.

And with any luck, Jeffie would dawdle on his way home. In fact, he'd no doubt stop by Dodge's place while Dodge was at the inn. "Did you lock your cabin?" she asked as he got in beside her.

"Yes. That's a custom computer I've got up there, to say nothing of the software project I'm working on."

That was all right then. Coffee let out a little breath of relief. Then perhaps this was as good a way of keeping the two of them apart as any. She'd just have to make sure that Dodge didn't stay too long. "You don't need to lock up in this town," she told him as the engine hummed to life and he pulled out onto the road. "But I'd appreciate it if you keep doing it."

His brows drew together as they reached the village and slowed for its quarter mile of shops, restaurants and strolling tourists. "Because of Jeff?"

She gave him a short nod, then slid lower in her seat as they passed the Ski Touring Center. Tongues wagged enough in this town already; no use giving them something as absurd as herself and Dodge to talk about.

Dodge let out a little hiss of exasperation. "You didn't answer my question last night. Why do you hate chess?"

Coffee hunched her shoulders. There was no way to tell him that, without telling him the heart of her secret. "I believe the deal was that I'd talk about Richard," she said coldly. "Not about me."

"The subjects seem pretty interconnected to me," he observed in as grim a voice. The Porsche growled past the little white clapboard schoolhouse where Jeffie would be finishing his day, then cut across the humped stone bridge in the center of town. Beneath its low arch, the Wildcat Brook was in full spate as it tumbled down from the falls a quarter mile above the bridge. Beyond the bridge, it ceased its headlong rush and widened to meander through the valley, as if it were reluctant to join the Ellis, a mile downstream. "If one were reduced to guessing," Dodge continued in a thoughtful voice as they followed the river uphill, "one could suppose that a petty, self-centered woman might be jealous of anything that distracted her husband from her own precious self. A woman like that wouldn't give a damn if chess made her husband happy...."

Was that how Dodge saw her? Coffee cast him a stricken look. Could that possibly be what she *was*—a petty, jealous woman? But no, if chess had made Richard happy... She'd never tried to stop him while he was driving toward the world championship. Sure, she'd been lonely, but she'd backed him every way she knew how in those years. It was after he'd won, when he'd come home so lost and confused, that she'd begun to realize what chess had done to him. And then, of course, once he was gone... "I'm not...like that," she said, shaking her head. "I'm not."

"No." Releasing the stick shift, Dodge brushed his knuckles along her cheek, then caught the wheel as they swooped around a rising curve. "I don't think you are, either."

Her skin tingling from that brief caress, she closed her eyes in momentary gratitude.

"So why do you hate chess?" he persisted.

He was driving after the answer the same way he'd have stalked the opposing king, with a feint from his knight on this side, a lunge from a bishop on that. And he'd keep on pressing until she gave him an answer. She let her breath out between her teeth. "I hate chess because it makes a person narrow—obsessive, all right? I don't want that for Jeffie. I want him to have friends, a wide range of interests. I don't want him to live like a little racehorse in blinders, only able to see and breathe and think one thing. There's so much *more* to life than just chess." There, would that satisfy him? But much as she believed what she'd said, she felt like a traitor to Richard for saying it to this man.

"Ah..." He drove in silence for a bit, then the curve at the corner of his mouth deepened. "So I suppose that explains me, too, since I've played chess all my life. Do you think I'm narrow?"

"I...don't know you that well," she hedged.

"Well, let's see... Besides playing chess I scuba dive, play raquetball, ski—alpine, not Nordic," he added quickly when she looked surprised. "I read fiction, collect oriental rugs, have friends all over the country, play the guitar pretty badly, cook pretty darn well if I do say so myself, run my own company and make it pay. I know all the major constellations, can whistle three octaves and I'm told I give a mean backrub." He shook his head, his mouth sorrowful, his eyes gleaming with laughter. "You're right, that's terribly narrow. I'd better pull up my socks and get busy."

She wanted to smile at his whimsical tone, but this was too important. "So that's you. But not everybody's like that."

"My point exactly, Coffee. And damn few are like Richard. There's no reason to suppose that Jeff—"

"There's *every* reason to suppose," she cut in. "He's Richard's son. I'm not about to risk it. I'm keeping Jeffie away from chess."

"You're not being reasonable," Dodge insisted as the Porsche swooped over the Owl Brook bridge, planks rumbling under its tires. "I agree with you that a child prodigy shouldn't have his little nose held to the grindstone, the way Richard's father—"

"Dodge, the subject is closed," Coffee snapped. The car turned into the parking lot and came to an abrupt halt before the inn. "I'll be the one to worry about Jeffie."

"And that's another thing," he growled, swinging to face her. "*Jeffie*. What are you trying to do, Coffee, curse the poor kid for life? It's time you started calling him Jeff. If his little friends hear you doing that—"

"Would you just mind your own business, Dodge?" Coffee fumbled for the release on her seat belt, but couldn't find it. She yanked off her mittens in disgust and tried again.

"What do you think I'm doing?" He swung out of his seat and stalked around the front of the car.

What did he mean by that? She stopped her struggles for a second to stare at him through the windshield. But before she had time to consider, the belt buckle parted beneath her fingers and she set the belt aside.

He opened the door for her as she turned, then offered his hand.

She didn't need that—didn't need his help at all, she told herself, but the reality was more basic than that. She didn't want to put her hand in his. Didn't want to see how small and delicate her fingers would look next to his, nor how much paler.

But when she swung her boots out to rest in the snow, he didn't back off, and his hand remained floating before her. *All right,* she thought, fuming, and accepted it. Hard and warm, his fingers closed around hers. She sucked in a tiny breath at the jolt of energy that sizzled up to her elbow. Color rising in her cheeks, she rose to face him.

His eyes seemed even blacker than usual. His lips moved slightly, but if it was a smile, he didn't complete it. "Why do we always end up fighting?" he asked huskily. His free hand came up to catch a strand of her hair as his fingers squeezed hers. "Hmm?" He tugged gently at the lock, letting it trail out between his fingertips like a ribbon of silk, then slid his hand beneath her hair and around to cradle the nape of her neck.

No, she couldn't let him kiss her. But she found herself leaning closer. "No," she said, her voice too soft and breathless.

His lips moved again, this time forming the hint of a smile. "No? And if I won't take no for an answer?"

"You'd better." She'd meant that as a command. It came out more like an appeal, begging to be brushed aside. The pressure on the back of her neck increased, and she tipped her head up in instinctive surrender.

And the storm door of the house squeaked open. Coffee flinched a half step backward as Dodge's fingers relaxed.

"Coffee?" Anke stood on the porch, frowning down at her anxiously. "Please to excuse me." Her blue eyes switched to Dodge, then back to Coffee's face, and her apple cheeks turned a charming pink. "But there is a phone call. I do not understand the man. And Maureen is sleeping."

"I'll be right there," Coffee replied, and she couldn't have said if she was grateful for the interruption or disappointed. But no, she would be crazy to fall for another game player. Just because she was vulnerable to him, it didn't follow that he felt anything at all for her, beyond the need to win the game. She'd learned that lesson too well. And besides, there was Jeffie to think about. She braced herself as Dodge turned back to face her and the door clicked shut behind Anke.

But that warm, irresistible intensity was gone from his face. In its stead his dark, straight brows had drawn together. "Who is that?" he demanded, jerking his chin at the house.

"That's Anke. Anke Meier. You met her the day Maureen fell down the stairs, remember?"

"Oh." There was a stillness about Dodge, as if he'd left his body behind to hold her hand, while his mind ranged somewhere miles away. "Right. She looks different when she's not hyperventilating. Who is she?"

"Dodge, I have somebody on the phone. Why don't you come in and ask her yourself, if you're so curious?" Her words came out sharper than she'd intended them. But a moment before, he'd looked as if he had nothing on his mind in all the world but the need to kiss her, and now he looked...stunned. Almost...smitten. She stared at him for an instant more, but he was hardly aware of her presence. His eyes were looking off over the river. Jerking her fingers from his, she hurried up the steps.

While she talked on the phone with the fuel-oil deliveryman, Dodge entered the inn. That startled look was gone now. Carrying his presents for Maureen and the scrapbook he was returning, he wore that bland expression he'd used on the doctor at the hospital. Coffee put a hand over the mouthpiece. "Maureen's asleep, Dodge."

"I can wait. Mind if I go get some coffee?"

Before she could even nod permission, he was striding off toward the kitchen. Which was where Anke had gone, Coffee was fairly certain. A faint buzz of voices from that direction confirmed it, then the voice nattering in her other ear drew her back to the matter at hand. "Let me check the fuel tanks and get back to you, can I, Ralph?" she appealed, but then Ralph wanted to tell her about his daughter's win in the slalom event the week before at Mount Cranmore.

It was a good ten minutes before Coffee managed to hang up. Biting her lip, she headed down the hall. Jeffie would be home any time now, and Dodge hadn't even started his visit with Maureen. But as she entered the kitchen, her steps faltered. Anke was sitting, facing Dodge at the big pine table. At Coffee's entrance, her head bobbed up like a startled deer's, then she jumped up from the table. Her porcelain complexion seemed even paler than usual, except for a fever spot of brilliant red on either cheek. Ducking her head, she hurried past Coffee. "Brigitta—it is time for her waking," she murmured, and darted out of the room.

There was no reason to feel sad, no reason to feel jealous, Coffee told herself as she hooked her thumbs into the pockets of her jeans. She'd done everything she could do to discourage Dodge, so she had no right to feel this way. If anything, she should be pleased to have her suspicions confirmed. Just a game player. *And any game will do, huh, fella?* But that was unfair; Anke was a very pretty woman. Peter had thought so as well, the instant he'd laid eyes on her.

Dodge picked up his mug from the table, drained it, then stood. "Well, what do you think? Is Maureen still sleeping?" He was wearing that bland look again, a butter-wouldn't't-melt expression that she bet he'd developed in his tournament years. Behind it, she could almost hear the wheels turning.

Well, fine. Let him think, let him fantasize. He was a free man, no concern of hers. "I'll go see," she said, and turned on her heel. Her hands were hurting, and as she walked, she glanced down at them in surprise. She was digging her nails into the palms.

While Dodge visited with Maureen, Coffee hovered in the kitchen. There was no tea to be served this afternoon, since the last of their guests had left this morning. But Jeffie would enter through the sunroom door when he came home. And she would whisk him straight up to his room on some pretext, though she had yet to think of anything plausible. She glanced at her watch. He must have stopped by Dodge's cabin. Could he simply be waiting on the deck for him there? But it was too cold outside to sit still for long. He'd have to give up and come home soon.

Pacing to the refrigerator, she opened the door and scowled at its contents. It was her night for cooking, since Anke had cooked last night.

"Coffee."

Dodge was lounging in the door to the hallway. He held another of Maureen's big red scrapbooks. That would be the one of Richard's middle years, no doubt. There was only one more. *Only three scrapbooks,* she thought; it wasn't enough for one lifetime. Suddenly her vision blurred and she spun away. Silly... she hadn't really cried for the last couple of years. Why was she so emotional nowadays? But the hand closing on her elbow told her why.

"Coffee?" He pulled her gently around in spite of her resistance. "What's the matter?"

"Nothing. I'm just being silly." She tried to laugh and failed miserably. "We're out of milk and mayonnaise and I hate to go shopping."

"You're—" He laughed, shook his head, then glanced down at the book he held and looked up again, instant comprehension driving the laughter from his eyes. "You really loved him," he said simply.

Which was the wrong thing to say. Her eyes filled again. And she wasn't even sure if that were so, anymore. She had cared—cared fiercely. Was that the same thing as love? Somehow, she was starting to think not. And if she hadn't really loved Richard, was that what had gone wrong? If she had, could she maybe have saved him? An arm hooked around her waist and drew her forward. She bumped into Dodge's shoulder and stood there, breathing deeply to banish the tears, inhaling the warm, seductive scent of his skin, of wool and a hint of bay rum. "Don't mind me, I'm just being foolish," she muttered against his shirt.

"There are worse things to be." His hand smoothed up her back, and he gave her a one-armed, soul-satisfying hug as he kissed the top of her head. "But it sounds like there's somebody on the porch. Jeff?" He let her go.

Wiping her face, Coffee turned as the door to the sunroom swung slowly open. She let out a gasp.

Wearing a brooding scowl, Jeffie peeked in through the widening gap. A trickle of dried blood ran from his pinkened nose down his face. More spatters of blood marked the white collar of his rugby shirt, and his hair stood up in tousled spikes. His hat was missing. As their eyes met, he winced and started to close the door, then stopped himself. His bottom lip pushing out even further, he shrugged and entered the room.

"*Jeffie!*" Dropping to her knees before him, Coffee caught him up in a passionate hug. "Baby, what happened?"

"Nothing!" he snarled, and tried to shrug out of her hold.

"Did you fall?"

His look of total disgust answered that question, but his bottom lip was starting to quiver and his eyes swam. If Coffee had known a way to press a button and make Dodge vanish from the face of the earth, or at least from this kitchen, she would have done so. Jeffie would die of mortification if he broke and started to cry now.

Dodge dropped on his heels beside her and held out a damp dish towel. "You took a good one, Jeff." His tone was matter-of-fact, almost but not quite admiring. Very masculine. "Looks like you get the purple heart."

"What's that?" Jeffie growled and took the towel automatically.

"When a soldier is wounded in the line of duty. It's a medal they give him." Dodge nudged the towel toward his face. "Now clean up. You're upsetting your mother."

Coffee sank back on her heels, looking from one to the other. Jeffie's scowl was starting to smooth away. He dabbed gingerly at his nose, and she fought back the temptation to take the towel and do it for him.

"What started it?" Dodge asked casually.

"Danny Lewis..." Jeffie mumbled, wincing as he scrubbed. "He said I was a liar. That I didn't drive your P-Porsche."

Danny Lewis! Why, he was almost two years older than Jeffie and much bigger! Then the rest of Jeffie's report hit home, and Coffee turned to stare at Dodge, her mouth agape.

But he ignored her. "Hope you set him straight on that."

"Yeah." Jeffie's scowl returned. "I tried."

"That's what counts." Dodge laid a finger alongside Jeffie's nose and frowned consideringly. "That hurt?"

"Uh-uh," Jeffie denied, though his eyes watered.

"Hmm. It's not swelling much. I don't think you broke it, this time."

This time! There wasn't going to be another, Coffee promised herself. Arlene Lewis wouldn't be home from work yet, but once she was, Coffee meant to have a word with her.

"Well." Dodge slapped Jeffie's shoulder briskly enough to rock him back on his heels. "Your shirt's a mess, pal. Better go change it."

"Yeah." Jeffie trudged off without even a glance for permission from Coffee.

"And Jeff?" Dodge's words stopped him in the doorway. He turned to look back at the man.

"I'm driving up to the base camp at Mount Washington tomorrow," Dodge said easily. "If you want to come along, I can pick you up...after school. I'll be parked out front by the fence. Okay?"

The look Jeffie gave him was one of purest bliss. "Okay." His shoulders straightened, then he ducked out of the room. *"Yeah!"* they heard him say to himself, as the implications began to hit home.

Dodge laughed under his breath, wadded the towel into a ball, then glanced at Coffee. He looked a little sheepish. "I didn't really let him drive. He just steered...on a straight-away...in first gear. I handled the pedals, of course."

Coffee wasn't sure if she wanted to kiss the man or explode.

"Well..." Dodge stood, then held out his hand. "Can you think of a better way to make Danny-boy eat his words?"

Coffee could not. But she'd been trying so hard to keep him and her son apart, and in one swoop, Dodge had blown that plan to smithereens. If she refused to let Jeffie go with him now, her son would never forgive her.

And worse yet was their destination. To Mount Washington... Absently accepting Dodge's hand, she rose from the floor and turned to face the distant mountain beyond the walls. With the sun setting it would be outlined in fire, while its sprawling bulk seemed to shadow half the world. She shivered suddenly and clasped her elbows to stop it.

"I won't talk about chess, Coffee, if it will make you any happier," Dodge promised behind her. "But at this age, the kid could use a little male companionship."

"Yes," she agreed absently, turning, but not yet seeing him. "But not you...." She shook her head, trying to shake a vision of snow falling on desolate rock out of her mind.

"I'm the only one who seems to be volunteering at the moment," Dodge growled. "Or is that so?"

She shrugged, hardly listening, and drifted toward the front door, hoping he'd follow. There was always Peter, of course, but Dodge was the only volunteer that Jeffie seemed to want. That was what frightened her so. For though Dodge promised not to talk about chess and she believed him, he was still a living, breathing reminder of the game to Jeffie.

With a hiss of exasperation, Dodge lifted the scrapbook off a counter and followed her down the corridor. They stopped by the front door. "I'd like your help with this scrapbook," Dodge said without compromise. "When can we get together? Tonight?"

No, she couldn't face him tonight. Coffee shook her head. She felt as if her nerves were stretched and quivering like the strings of a violin in his presence. Pluck them one more time today and something would snap.

"Tomorrow night? I'll have Jeff back no later than four. If you wanted to come out, catch a bite to eat somewhere..." Dodge's chin lifted as footsteps sounded on the stairs. Anke was descending, Gitta balanced on her hip. Her face was very pale and her expression almost defiant as she looked down at Dodge. Then her eyes moved to Coffee. "Jeffie... you have seen his poor nose?"

"Yes, I'm just going up to him," Coffee assured her. Beside her, Dodge had gone stone-still.

As Anke reached the ground floor, Dodge's hand rose as if to stop her. Instead, he touched Gitta's cheek. "Pretty child," he said in an expressionless voice.

Anke's face flushed as if a sun had risen inside her. "Thank you." She hurried on down the hallway without a backward glance.

Unsmiling, unblinking, Dodge looked after her until she vanished into the family room. Then with a tiny jerk of his head, he turned back to Coffee. "Well..." But his eyes were looking right through her. "I'll... call you." Absently, he touched her shoulder, then let himself out the door.

Slowly Coffee closed it behind him. He'd forgotten to set their next date to look at the scrapbook. Or was it that he just didn't care?

So why should she? Why, oh, why should she? Squaring her shoulders, Coffee hurried up the stairs.

CHAPTER NINE

"DA!"

"Yes, that's a dog," Maureen agreed, smiling down at the child curled in the big easy chair beside her.

Gitta patted the book's illustration again. "Da! Da!" She laughed excitedly, then, sticking out her lower lip in concentration, the child turned the page.

"She's going to be speaking English in no time," Maureen assured Coffee, who was poking at the logs in the fireplace. "And that fire was burning perfectly fine, thank you. Can't you sit still for a minute? You're worse than Miss Wigglewart here."

"Sorry," Coffee muttered, but Maureen's attention had already switched back to Gitta, who was patting the picture before them.

"Vis?" she demanded. "Vis?"

"That's a kitty cat," Maureen said, and apparently that was the question, because Gitta nodded with vast satisfaction.

Smiling in spite of her worries, Coffee left them to it and prowled out of the room. Pausing in the doorway, she swung back to consult the mantel clock. Nearly four. She'd have to leave soon, whether Dodge had brought Jeffie back by then or not.

Pacing down the hallway to the front desk, she poked at the stacks of envelopes that held a year's tax receipts for the Owl Brook Inn. Yesterday, when Dodge had pressed her for a meeting tonight, she'd forgotten that she had an appointment scheduled with the bed and breakfast's accountant in North Conway. But she didn't want to leave for that meeting until she'd seen Jeffie safely back from his expedition to Mount Washington.

Crossing her arms and hugging herself, she wandered back down the hall and into the kitchen. The door to the sunroom was open—a waste of heat at this time of day, when the sun had already sunk behind the mountains. Coffee walked over to it, started to close it, then instead restlessly stepped out into the room.

Dustcloth in hand, Anke stood transfixed before the framed family photographs that decorated one wall. Her nose only inches from the glass, she was staring at one of Coffee's favorites. It was a picture Maureen had taken the day she, Coffee and Jeffie—age two at the time—had driven down to the airport in Boston to collect Richard. After nearly two months away, he'd been returning from a tournament in Brazil. Standing beside Coffee, Jeffie riding his shoulders, he looked tanned, handsome, all that a young husband should have been. It was one of the few pictures Coffee had of him smiling. One of the few pictures of the three of them together.

At the sound of Coffee's footsteps, Anke jumped and looked around.

"You've found the family mug shots," Coffee said to break the silence.

"Ah..." Anke said on an uncomprehending note, her startled look of guilt beginning to fade. She smiled apologetically. "This is...was...your husband?" She tapped the photo's glass with a fingernail.

"Yes." Coffee came to stand beside her. "That's Richard...."

Anke let out a little sigh. "He looks very...happy."

"Yes." Coffee smiled to herself. Cock-a-hoop was more like it. "He'd just won an important tournament." He'd defeated a former world champion, also a Russian, in that match, and had come back sure that he could take the present champion. Not that he'd ever had any doubts.

"Ah..." Anke said again. "And you look happy, too."

Coffee studied the photo. "Yes, I guess I do." She was looking up at Richard, startled, as she'd always been on his returns, at how much taller he was in reality than in her memory. She remembered she'd been very proud of him, and a bit shy, as if this were a stranger she'd be taking home to her bedroom that night. But, yes, she'd been glad to have him back.

"You loved him," Anke said on a note of discovery.

"That's what husbands are for," Coffee said, too lightly. But she didn't want to think of Richard. Would he ever let her go? Was it love that was binding her so tightly to his memory, or guilt that she hadn't been able to save him? And either way, did it matter? She couldn't quite seem to cut the strings and go on. Maybe that was because the one man who might have tempted her to try again was the same man who kept dragging her back to confront her old ghosts.

Willing herself to sidestep that train of thought, she glanced at the woman beside her. "And your husband, Anke, where is he?" It was a question she'd been wanting to ask for days.

She regretted it immediately. The blonde's pale complexion turned a fiery red to the hairline. "There...is no husband," she said, refusing to meet Coffee's eyes. She stared past her at the photos. "There never was."

That was what Coffee had half suspected. Not that it mattered to her in the least. She'd seen enough in the last few days to know that whatever the situation had been, Anke had played an honorable part in it, if one could use such an old-fashioned word. But then Anke was endearingly old-fashioned, it sometimes seemed. "I'm sorry," she said simply.

Anke turned to look at her directly. "There is no need to be sorry," she said with an almost fierce dignity.

"No need at all," Coffee agreed, "unless you're sorry. Then I'm sorry, too." She touched Anke's arm. "That's what friends are for."

The young woman might have been translating those words into German, she took so long to react to them. Then a warm, shy smile spread slowly across her face. "Yes...."

Coffee returned that smile as long as she could, and then, as if the move had been choreographed, they turned as one to the photos.

"Did you see this one of Peter?" Coffee asked at random. "I took that at the Fireman's Barbecue, in the park last Labor Day. He's one of our volunteer firemen, you know?"

"Yes, he told me. But what is he doing?"

"He was playing air guitar for us." Coffee laughed, remembering. Seeing Anke's puzzled face, she had to explain. In the middle of it, she turned at the sound of galloping footsteps, then Jeffie burst into the sunroom.

"Mommy! We're back!" he cried and caught her hand. "Dodge bought me a T-shirt, see?" He pulled open his jacket to show her a shirt with a pen-and-ink design of a rabbit on the front. "And Danny Lewis and the other guys saw me get in the Porsche!" He did a little hopping dance of glee. "I gotta tell Gram!" He stopped as Dodge appeared in the doorway. "She's out here," he announced, then ducked under Dodge's elbow and disappeared.

"So I see..." Dodge lounged in the doorway, his red parka slung over one shoulder. He smiled at them both. "Hello."

Anke murmured something about Gitta and hurried toward him, her eyes downcast.

Whatever his interest had been in the blonde the day before, it seemed to have waned. He gave her a polite smile, nothing more, as he stepped out of her way, then moved to fill the doorway again.

And it was time for her to be going as well, Coffee realized. But she stood where she was, her chin up, her breath coming a little faster than it had a moment ago. What was it about this man? There were plenty of handsome men in a resort town like Jackson, so why this one?

"Tonight?" he asked, resuming the conversation exactly where he'd left it the day before. "We can check out a restaurant, something down in North Conway if you like, then—" He stopped as she shook her head.

"I'm afraid I have a previous date, Dodge." She liked the way his brows drew together at that, so much that she couldn't resist adding, "With the most important man in the world to me...."

"Oh?" He looked half wary, half suspicious that he was being teased as he stepped down to the sunroom. "Who's the lucky guy?"

"My tax accountant. He plays my hero once a year, and tonight's his night."

Dodge's face relaxed slowly into a smile. "I see.... Well, let's hope he comes through for you. In that case, tomorrow. I'll pick you up at six."

"Okay...." She wanted, almost needed, to spread her hand on his chest. In her mind's eye she could see her hand resting there, see it sliding sideways beneath his shirt. That dark swirl of hair that was just peeking out the vee of his collar would feel like silk beneath her fingertips. She tore her eyes away. "Want to walk out with me? I'm late already."

They walked in silence down the hall, and though it was a wide one, they bumped shoulders gently, three times, between the kitchen and the front desk. She picked up her records, then Dodge held the door for her.

"See you tomorrow then," he said, his smile lighting his eyes.

"You're not going, too?" Startled, she stopped halfway out the door.

"Nope, figured I'd stay and chat a while with Maureen."

"But Jeffie—" She stopped, confused. Just because she found Dodge's company more and more enticing didn't mean that she was comfortable with the thought of—

His mouth hardened. "Coffee..." He shook his head. "I thought I'd broken that hex. You trusted me with him all afternoon."

"You didn't give me much choice, did you?" she reminded him. His fingers tightened on the door next to her face. He was madder than he looked, she realized, glancing up at his white knuckles.

"No, I guess I didn't," he said dryly. "Well, you're going, and I'm staying. So what do you want me to do? Talk to Maureen, but cut Jeff dead every time he speaks to me? Or would you prefer to take him with you?"

"Neither of those choices will work, and you know it, Dodge."

"I know it. Now if *you'd* just figure that out." He shrugged, his face relaxing into ruefulness. "Coffee, I swear the word *chess* will never cross my lips tonight. They are sealed." He ran a fingertip along her mouth, from one corner to the other then back again, as if demonstrating. "There, now may I go see Maureen?"

He had her, of course. She gave him a short nod, then slipped out the door and let him close it. Her hands full of tax records, she stood very still for a minute, staring out the storm door, her lips still quivering from his touch, and then swung back. Returning to the front door, she leaned closer to peer through a clear spot between two etched swirls of glass.

Dodge stood at the far end of the hall. His arms crossed, he was lounging against the wall, his head tipped down as he spoke. And before him stood Anke, an uncertain smile flitting across her pretty face.

Was that why he'd been so anxious to stay? If her hands had not been full, Coffee would have touched her lips. She could not quite believe that a moment ago he'd caressed them, and now— Then Jeffie popped out of the family room and beamed up at Dodge as he spoke. Clapping him on the shoulder, Dodge said a last word to Anke, then followed Jeffie back into the room. With a soft sigh of bewilderment, Coffee turned and went.

SKIING WAS A GOOD antidote to confusion. The next day, after she'd finished her morning chores, Coffee took to the trails. It was one way of driving Dodge Phillips out of her mind. If she didn't know what she wanted, what he wanted, what she should or could do to protect Jeffie, at least she could stop spinning her mental wheels and get some exercise.

So stop thinking about him, she told herself for the fiftieth time as she glided toward the little path that led down from his cabin. But glancing up it as she passed, she spread her skis and slid to a stop.

Someone had come down that trail—sometime today, since it had snowed almost four inches during the night. Could Jeffie have stopped by Dodge's cabin on his way to school? She bit her lip in thought, then shook her head. The trail wasn't that steep. He would have snowplowed at the top there, coming around that turn, then again as he turned out onto the main trail. But in between he would have simply tucked low and enjoyed the descent, his skis parallel. She knew her daredevil son.

And besides... She smiled suddenly. Ten feet above the intersection of the trails, off to one side of the smaller path, there was a wide patch of thrashed and flattened snow. Someone had taken a fall there. Her smile widened. *Couldn't be,* she told herself as she pushed off and started downhill again. *Could be anyone.* Still... the day seemed suddenly a little brighter, the air in her lungs effervescent with cold and the tang of pine resin.

Tucking down over her skis as the trail sharpened, her poles cocked up behind her, she kept her eyes peeled. She shot past two more fall spots, snowplowed around a steeper drop, and found Dodge at the bottom of that pitch, leaning against a tree, his poles propped out to either side.

It was pure showboating to do a telemark stop beside him, but she did it anyway, showering his boots with a little wave of fresh snow. "Hiya!"

"Hi." For once he didn't look glad to see her, but his eyes flicked down the taut line of her body to her skintight ski pants, then back up again.

Perhaps it was that almost unwilling inspection, perhaps the sense of freedom and power that she always felt on skis, or perhaps some inner devil—wherever the impulse came from, she reached up to brush the telltale snow off his shoulders and cap. "Having fun?" she teased.

"Barrels," he growled. "I woke up this morning, saw all that fresh snow and decided it'd be a great day to go out and hold up a tree." He patted the birch he was leaning against. "Meanwhile, don't let me interrupt you. You were going someplace."

"Oh... I'm in no hurry." Suddenly, there was no place she'd rather be.

"What I was afraid of." His mouth twitched in spite of himself, and he pushed away from the tree to stand sideways to the slope. "Scratch a gorgeous blonde, you find a sadist every time. So what'll it be? A pratfall or a nosedive, or shall I simply break my neck for your viewing pleasure?"

She laughed and shook her head. "Why didn't you sign up for lessons at the Ski Touring Center when you rented your skis?"

"I figured anybody who could ski downhill could handle cross-country."

Coffee smiled. She'd heard that same note of indignation from many a disillusioned downhill hotshot. "Both sports use snow, true, but the technique isn't quite the same."

"Tell me about it!"

She slid one ski back and forth, then the other, in a joyful little snow dance. "Want a lesson, or would you rather slog on without witnesses?" She held her breath. He'd been in control of every encounter they'd had so far. Was he secure enough to let a woman take the lead?

His eyebrows lifted, then dropped in a shrug of resignation. "Looks like I need one."

"Okay." She stopped smiling, though the smile felt as if it had settled somewhere behind her heart, and automatically dropped into her teaching persona—brisk and optimistic, someone who wouldn't dream of laughing out loud when her pupil ate snow. "Since we're already on a slope, I guess we'd better start with the snowplow. So... just watch me do one.... Notice that I'll actually lift one ski out of the track so that's it's easier to push it out to the side...."

He was a fast learner with good balance. Gradually, as Dodge stopped fighting the skis and accepted the fact that he hadn't the precision control afforded by downhill boot bindings, he began to improve. Encouraging him and offering mild critiques, Coffee led him to the north, away from the village. She told herself that he'd want to be challenged, that he'd easily become bored on the nearly horizontal skiing down in the valley. But though that was true, whether she could admit it or not, there were other reasons.

Even in midweek the beginner courses were always in use, and she didn't want to share his company with another soul. It was nicer out here in the pine-scented silence, where the only sound was their breathing, or the slither and *thump* of a pine branch shedding its load of snow.

And she also liked the fact that on the tougher slopes he was slightly overextended and knew it. He didn't feel so threatening out here in her home territory. "We'll have to herringbone to the top of this one," she told him as he joined her at the base of a hill.

"Fine, you go right ahead," he told her and stuck his poles upright in the snow. "I'm going to stand here and cool off." He was fast learning what a warm sport ski touring was. He'd already shed his parka and his cap, stuffing them into the backpack that Coffee wore when she skied, and beneath his tan, his face had a fine healthy flush across the cheekbones.

"Okay." They'd have a drink at the top, Coffee promised herself as she duck-walked up the slope. She was feeling pretty warm herself, though she was down to her wool shirt and her usual lace undershirt of polypropylene. Halfway up she stopped, panting, to look over her shoulder.

Dodge had unbuttoned his shirt and pulled it out of his waistband. He was gaining on her, his superior strength counterbalancing her skill. "You're going to freeze to death next time you stop," she called, laughing.

"Huh! It's up to ninety at least," he gasped.

And he drank as if it were high noon in the desert when he joined her at the top of the run and she handed him her water bottle. He closed his eyes and swallowed, a trickle of water running down the side of his damp throat, then into the dark hair that swirled across his broad chest. Fascinated, Coffee drank in the spectacle. He was beautiful, hard without being overbuilt. And though he hadn't mentioned lifting weights when he'd listed his accomplishments the other day, he must surely be doing so. Perhaps he didn't think of that as a hobby, but merely routine, like brushing teeth or watching one's diet. She'd have liked to ask, but couldn't think of a way to phrase it that wouldn't tell him she'd noticed.

But mesmerized as she was by the sight of him, her discretion was wasted. She looked up from his chest to find he was now watching *her*. Taking the bottle he offered, she looked quickly away again, the color rising in her cheeks.

"Well..." She jammed the bottle into her hip holster and started out. But the trail was wider here. Dodge caught up and skied alongside. She glanced at him sideways. His eyes were very dark, very intent upon her. She suddenly wished she'd not undone the top two buttons of her shirt, which was silly, considering that she knew experienced skiers who, as they heated up, skied the backwoods in nothing but their long johns. "How's the research coming?" she asked, simply to break the uneasy silence.

"Coming along. I've been analyzing Richard's moves in his pivotal games for the last year, so I know what I'll write for those chapters. And I've been reviewing the definitive biographies on Fischer, Karpov and the other giants these last few weeks. All I have to do is finish my notes on Maureen's scrapbooks and ask you a few more questions.''

And then his research would be done, and he would go. While she—she would stay here, following the endless cycle of her days at the bed and breakfast, a routine that had once seemed all she needed. And when the loneliness of that overwhelmed her, she could take her sadness to the mountains and ski these trails. But in the end, they would only lead her back to a place that would now, after Dodge, seem empty. Without a heart. *I need a man to love,* she thought, and skied faster. *I need someone to need me.* Not the way that Jeffie and Maureen needed her, but the way a man needed a woman.

But it wouldn't be this man. He might want her, but he hadn't offered his love, and if he had, it wouldn't work. Because there was Jeffie to consider. Jeffie came first, no matter how lonely she might be. So it couldn't be this man.

She could almost hate him for that. Dodge had awakened this yearning in her, a thirst as unquenchable as Jeffie's thirst for chess. And soon he would go, leaving her to cope alone with both her own unsatisfied needs and those of her son. "So why don't you ask your blasted questions and get it over with?" she panted.

"Right now?"

"Why not?" The pain would only grow, the longer he stayed.

"When I'm dying of heat stroke and you're skiing my legs off?" When she nodded without looking at him, he caught her arm and pulled her to a halt. "Whatever you say, lady. If you're in the mood, you're in the mood."

She had wanted to talk while they traveled, not standing here where she had to look him in the eye. But it was too late now.

"All right," Dodge said, breathing hard. "I want to know. Why did Richard quit chess after the championship? I can't write the book without knowing that."

She'd been a idiot to invite this. She swung away, but he caught her shoulder and turned her back again. "Why, Coffee?" he insisted.

She could hear her heart pounding—it still thought she was skiing. Somewhere off in the forest, a bird was calling *hee yee yee,* in a bittersweet, tiny voice. Behind Dodge stood a massive birch, its silvery bark scarred and filigreed with nets of black. Where a branch had long since fallen away, the dark lines grew in a concentric circle, forming a wrinkled, sardonic eye that watched her over his shoulder. "Why?" Dodge asked. "It was all that he knew how to do. Why would he quit?" Far away and sad, the bird cried again.

"I...don't know," she said, and tried to swallow the lump in her throat.

"Coffee..." He shook his head, not believing her.

"I *don't.* He wouldn't talk about it." After he'd returned from Berlin he'd simply brooded, or had disappeared for days at a time to ski in the mountains, then eat and sleep in the climbers' dormitory at the Mount Washington base camp. Whenever she'd tried to ask him what was wrong, he'd simply snarled at her.

Dodge put a hand on her shoulder. "Were you two having...problems?"

"Yes! Okay, we were." She looked away, then swung back again. "Are you going to put that in your book?"

"I'm just trying to understand." His fingers tightened until they almost hurt her. "Tell me this...if he'd lived, would you have left him?"

She stood very still, her eyes unfocused as if she were listening. Would she have? Oh, she'd wanted to.... Those last months after he'd returned had been terrible. For years she'd been telling herself that everything would come out right once he'd accomplished his goal and come home to stay. Instead she'd found herself all the lonelier, having him home and yet finding they were no closer. Lying by her side, or sitting silently across the breakfast table from her, Richard had been as remote as if he'd stayed in Berlin.

But would she have divorced him? "No...." It wasn't in her to turn her back on the man she'd promised to love, but oh, the terrible relief at the end when she thought he'd turned his back on her. When he'd said, "Coffee, it's over."

"No," she said again, but it was more a protest at the memories unfolding within her than an answer to Dodge's question. Wrenching away from his hold, she set out again at a pace he'd not be able to match.

Richard had locked himself in his little study all that last morning, and when he'd come out at last, he'd been carrying the backpack that held his winter camping gear. But this time she'd run out of patience. She'd been determined not to let him go, determined that this time he must face her. This time she absolutely *had* to find out what was going through his head. But he'd listened in stony silence until she'd argued and pleaded herself to a standstill, then had started once more for the door.

"*Richard!*" she'd called after him, half in anger, half in despair. If he wouldn't even try...

Turning to look back at her, his face as cold and remote as the mountains toward which he was heading, he'd simply said, "Coffee, its over." Then he'd walked out the door.

And God forgive her, she'd thought he meant their marriage, and the first emotion she'd felt was relief.

That was the first emotion; shock and hurt had stumbled immediately on its heels. And it had been pride that had made her shrug, then call after him, "Whatever you say!"

So she had stood there and let him walk out of the house on that brilliant, frigid morning, had watched numbly from the window as he'd skied down the hill. And she'd never once dreamed what he had really meant by those words.

It was only two days later, when she'd driven up to the base camp at Mount Washington, assuming that that was where Richard had been sleeping and determined that they talk, that she'd had the first inkling of what he might really have meant. For no one at the base camp had seen Richard that week.

Once she'd learned that, she'd told herself that he'd left the valley, had probably hitchhiked down to North Conway, then caught a bus to New York to stay with his father. But still she'd gone to Peter for advice. And it turned out that the ski patrolman had passed Richard two days before, heading north up the Ellis River Trail toward Mount Washington.

So Peter had called out the search teams, and at first everyone had been cautiously optimistic. The weather had been fine if bitterly cold, and Richard was an experienced winter camper with top-notch gear. He should have been able to survive two days out on the mountain.

But only hours after the search began, one of those sudden, devastating storms for which Mount Washington was notorious had swept in on the jet stream, then wrapped its purple clouds around the mile-high peak. The blizzard had driven the searchers down below the timberline, then all the way down the mountain to the safety of the valley. A week later, when the storm had blown itself out, they had resumed the search, but this time without hope.

By then, Maureen had found the letter Richard had left behind, and Coffee had already known the worst. She knew that he'd been talking about his life, not their marriage, when he'd said, "It's over."

Behind her, so close that she jumped, another man's voice cut through the bitter memories. "Coffee, slow down!"

Instead of slowing, she ducked her head and stretched out until she was almost flying. She couldn't face Dodge right now. He'd have to ski home alone. She didn't doubt for a moment that he could do so.

"Damn it, Coffee! You've got my trail map! And my jacket!"

She'd forgotten. Ahead on the trail, a mound of snow had sifted off an overhanging fir to half block the way. She lifted her left ski over it, set it down again, then glanced behind. Dodge was striding hot on her trail, his face dark with irritation and the effort of keeping up with her.

"Coffee!" he yelled on a note of clear warning, just as his ski tip caught the mound of snow. His left ski stopped while the rest of him continued its forward rush.

"Dodge!"

For an endless moment he was airborne, poles flailing like useless wings, skis clattering behind him. Then he hit the edge of the trail in an explosion of powder snow.

"Dodge!" His head only inches from the trunk of a pine, he lay face down, spread-eagled, utterly motionless after all that terrible motion. At the very least, with his nose buried he'd smother. Releasing her bindings, Coffee leaped out of her skis and ran to kneel beside him.

But there was no way to turn him over while he was attached to his skis. Frantically, she popped the catches on his bindings and threw the skis aside.

"Dodge!" She didn't want to move him, but oxygen had to come first, any broken bones later. Catching his shoulder and the hard angle of his hipbone, she rolled him over.

His eyes were closed, his black, thick lashes fringed with snow. His bare chest was slick with sweat and the snow melted by his overheated skin. "Dodge!" She brushed snow off his face, touched his heaving chest. He was alive, but if she couldn't revive him out here... God, she'd been a selfish idiot! Struggling out of her backpack, she yanked out his parka, spread it over his chest, then cupped his face with her hands. "Dodge?"

The dark lashes fluttered, but his eyes didn't open. Gently she began to explore his skull beneath the thick, soft hair, then his neck, searching its hard, smooth length for any sign of injury. But she could find nothing amiss. "Dodge?" Pushing the parka down, she explored his collarbones, but the elegant, almost sculptural forms were perfectly symmetrical. At a loss, she laid her hand over his heart, felt it slamming against her palm, then jumped as his hand swung up to pin hers in place. "Oh!"

"You're not going to try mouth-to-mouth resuscitation?" he inquired as he opened his eyes.

"You're all right!" she gasped, and tried to sit back on her heels. But his hand tightened over her fingers, keeping her where she was.

"Not as right as I'd have been if you'd fallen for that one." He was starting to grin.

And she was starting to get angry, he'd frightened her so. "*Damn* it, Dodge!"

"Damn it, yourself. What were you planning to do, leave me out here to wander till I froze?"

It was too like her recent thoughts. There hadn't been a mark on Richard when they found him in the spring, high up the mountain in a natural amphitheater called the Gulf of Slides. Had he climbed till he could climb no more? Or had he simply sat and waited for the cold to take him? She would never know. She shuddered violently, her mouth opening, then closing again as no words came to mind.

His smirk faded as he watched her face. "I'm sorry...."

She shook her head, trying to smile. It was hardly his fault.

"Looks like you're the one who needs a little resuscitation," he continued huskily. Half sitting, Dodge stuffed the parka beneath him, then hooked an arm around her waist. He lay back again, pulling her down with him to cradle her against his bare chest.

"No..." she protested, but her fingers had spread against the warm, resilient contours of his body and seemed to have fused there.

"*Yes.*" Cupping one hand to her face, he coaxed her mouth down to his. "It's a nice word, Coffee," he murmured, lipping her as he spoke. "It's high time you tried it." His fingers twisted sensuously into her hair, gathering it at the nape of her neck. Outlining her mouth with just the tip of his tongue, he was asking for entry, not demanding it.

Yes...he was right. When had she last said yes to life? Yes to such pleasure. To such gentle, heartbreaking strength as these arms that now held her. Oh, she needed this—needed him. With a hungry little sigh, she surrendered her mouth to his.

He groaned deep in his throat, a very masculine sound of triumph and release, then entered her in a kiss that was a joining more than a caress. His hands stroked from her hips to her head and back again, molding her to him, while their tongues spoke their own silent language of joy. With a murmur of delight, Coffee snuggled closer, wrapped her arms tightly around his neck—and felt them sink into the snow. "Dodge!" She tore her mouth away. "You must be freezing." The parka had slipped, and his wool shirt was not protection at all from the snow beneath.

"Freezing?—I'm going to go up in a puff of smoke!" He kissed her chin, the line of her jaw, the hollow at the base of her throat, the lace where the lapels of her shirt met in a vee.

"You can't lie in the snow." They were miles from home, and he was a beginner skier who'd just taken a bad fall. Let him get chilled and he'd grow even clumsier.

"So I'll sit up." Suiting action to words, he reached for her again.

One more kiss, then she would get him moving again. But there was no line of demarcation. One kiss flowed into the next, became a liquid, molten stream of bliss, a tactile language of question and shuddering response, a breathless rushing toward knowledge and delight. She should stop him, but no one had ever kissed her eyelids before, and once he'd done so, she couldn't conceive of anyone but Dodge ever kissing them again.

But he's going. Arching her neck as his lips wandered down her throat to her shoulder, gasping at the starburst of sensations radiating out from his kisses, she stared wide-eyed at the branches above. He was going, once he'd finished his research. And she was staying. She let out a pleading cry as his teeth closed gently in the top of her shoulder, and hugged him even closer.

She would be staying here in Jackson, remembering the way he'd kissed her, and never wanting another man to touch her again because of the way this man had made her feel. *Stop this before it's too late,* she told herself frantically. This wasn't heaven they were rushing toward, but heartache. "Stop!" she murmured against his mouth.

"Hmm?" He backed off an inch or two to see her eyes, but his hand spanned her throat and stroked upward, tipping her chin for his next kiss.

"We've got to stop." Though, oh, she didn't want to. But that was the clearest warning of all that she *must* stop this. She ran a hand across his chest and felt him shudder. "You must be freezing. This is crazy."

"Crazy? This is the first time we've made sense, Coffee." He stroked his thumb across her bottom lip, coaxing her mouth open. "I'm afraid if we stop..." But he shivered again.

This time her concern was all for him. "We've got to." She glanced to the west. Once the sun dipped behind the mountains, the temperature would plummet. She had to get him home. "On your feet, soldier!" She scrambled to her own, and held out her hand to him.

He caught it, but made no motion to rise. "Guess you're right." He took a deep breath, visibly reaching for control, then his fingers tightened on hers. "Besides, I've got a hot date at six."

She'd forgotten that. But she couldn't go through with that now, couldn't let herself be alone with Dodge again. One more kiss like the last one and she wouldn't melt—she'd burst into flames. There was a certain self-limiting safety to kissing him in the middle of a snowbank, come to think of it. She shook her head. "I don't really think—"

"That's what I was afraid of," he cut in, his mouth wry. "But think again." Without pulling on her hand, he rose to his feet.

"I have." She couldn't be alone with him in his cabin, not after this. They'd opened a door that she'd not be able to close again, and he knew it as well as she did. "I can't. I just can't, Dodge."

Lifting her hand, he set it over his heart. "Can't, Coffee, or won't?"

Belying the calmness of his voice, his heart was slamming against his ribs. Like an echo, her own heartbeat answered it, drumming its own song of desire in her ears.

"It doesn't much matter, does it?" she asked dully while she fought the urge to knead his skin with her fingertips. She couldn't betray her own need for lasting love as well as present sexual delight. And even if he'd offered her more than a "hot date," she wouldn't betray Jeffie by loving a man who would endanger him. "It comes out to the same thing in the end."

"Oh, it matters a lot, Coffee," Dodge disagreed. "One I might get around. The other..." He shrugged. Dropping her hand, he reached for his shirt and began buttoning it. "Cold out here," he muttered, his dark eyes looking right through her. "Too damn cold."

Yes, she could feel the bitter chill seeping into her heart. For just a moment she'd thought she was glimpsing a tenderness she'd never known before, a tenderness so great that it could trap her and possess her forever. But she'd been wrong—he'd been offering her passion, not tenderness. It had been just a game, that was all, and now that he'd lost, he wasn't even being a good sport about it.

They skied back in the same frosty silence, Coffee in the lead, Dodge following, his face distant and thoughtful every time she looked back at him. As they neared the cabin from the road side, Dodge skied ahead and led the way around back to the stairs leading up to his deck.

"Well..." Coffee stabbed the blue-shadowed snow with her pole tip as Dodge stepped out of his bindings. She didn't know what to say. She wanted some healing between them, but could think of no words that would effect it. Though she owed him no apology, she wanted to offer one. It wouldn't have been made with words; she'd have simply stepped into his arms and offered her lips. But that was a crazy impulse. That was what had caused all this bad feeling already. If she hadn't let him start, he wouldn't be so angry that she hadn't or wouldn't let him finish. "Well," she said again.

Did he still want her help with the scrapbooks? And if he did, would he consent to meet her someplace safe? Perhaps a restaurant for lunch? Or would that suggestion just make him angry all over again?

"Well..." Dodge propped his skis against the stair railing. "Do you want to come in?"

He knew the answer to that. Her sadness shifted toward irritation as she shook her head.

"No? Not even with a chaperon?" Dodge jerked a thumb at the cords of split wood stacked below the deck, and Coffee's eyes followed the gesture to a pair of small skis propped against the logs. Jeffie's skis.

Heart sinking, she glanced overhead at the deck, but if Jeffie were waiting there, he'd have sung out by now. "You didn't lock up today?"

"Looks like I forgot." Dodge didn't even have the grace to seem regretful, but his smile held a touch of bitterness she'd not seen before. With a careless shrug, he started up the stairs.

He had turned her life upside down since his coming. She couldn't begin to think how she'd ever put it right once he was gone. But the sooner he was gone, the sooner she could start mending her heart and her world. Releasing her bindings with two jabs of a pole tip, she bounded up the stairs after him and caught his arm. "Dodge, when are you leaving?"

His face went blank as he looked down at her. "That's what you want?"

No! she almost cried out. No, it was the last thing in the world she wanted, but it was what she and Jeffie needed.

As the silence stretched between them, his mouth twisted. "When, Coffee?" he asked, anger simmering behind the words. "When I find the answer to one more question—not a minute before. So you'd better get used to it." Shaking her hand off, he turned and continued up the stairs. "Coming?" he added mockingly, without looking back.

With Jeffie up there? He knew she was. But what his question was, or its answer, she could no more have said than what she was feeling at this moment. *He wasn't leaving yet.* With hope and fear at war in her heart, she followed him up the stairs.

CHAPTER TEN

THROUGH THE SLIDING GLASS door Coffee could see Jeffie, perched on the edge of Dodge's coffee table. Utterly absorbed, he was staring down at a tournament-size chess set. As she sucked in her breath, he lifted a black rook off the game board before him, moved it to a new position, then rotated the board so that now he was his own opponent, playing white. He picked up the white queen, moved it two squares ahead, then spoke aloud. Though his voice did not reach her through the glass, his lips were easy to read. The word had been "check."

"You see!" she whispered furiously.

"I see a kid doing something he loves," Dodge retorted. He caught her arm as she started forward and swung her to face him, catching her other arm to hold her there. "Coffee, look. I don't know what you're so afraid of, but you've got nothing to fear."

"You don't understand!" she cried, then regretted the words immediately.

"I'm trying to." His hands tensed, effortlessly holding her in place as she tried to twist out of his grip. "God *knows* I'm trying to, but you're fighting me every step of the way." He gave her an exasperated little shake, but when he spoke again, his voice held the weight and deliberation of someone determined to make his point. "Look . . . I think one of the most important things a man—a person—has to do in life is find something he does well. There's a kind of joy in that, Coffee. You know that—I've watched your face when you ski. Well, that's what's pulling Jeff. He's found what he does well." His hands gentled on her arms, his thumbs moving in a restless, unconscious caress. His eyes were locked on hers as if he could persuade her through the intensity of his gaze alone. "And I wonder what happens to a person if you thwart such a talent? Does the person—does Jeff—find something else that he loves to do? Or does something break inside, Coffee? Does he just wander aimlessly for the rest of his life, looking and never finding?"

She shuddered and shook her head. Of course she didn't want that for Jeffie. She wanted him to have something he loved, but not something that could maim and even kill. But if Dodge were right, if the denying of Jeffie's talent could also maim...

"You're worrying too much," Dodge continued earnestly. "The only way chess is going to turn into an obsession for Jeff is if you insist on snatching it away from him. You've never heard about forbidden fruit tasting the sweetest?"

He was hitting every nail of her fear squarely on its head. But still... She turned her head to watch Jeffie move another chessman. "Look at him, Dodge. He's off in another world. He should know we're out here. We're not whispering."

"The kid's got wonderful concentration," Dodge agreed. "Nothing wrong with that. It doesn't mean he'll always concentrate on chess." His hands slid down from her arms to lock behind her waist, and he pulled her forward. "Look, trust me for once. Let's not make a big deal of this, okay? I agree that all chess and no play makes Jack a dull boy. So let's do something besides chess tonight. Hmm?" Arching her even closer, he rubbed the tip of his nose up the curve of hers to her eyebrows, then nuzzled them with a playful tenderness that clutched at her heart. "What do you say?" he coaxed, his lips skimming her face. "We can cook supper—I've got a steak in the fridge. Then we'll catch an early movie in North Conway. We can have him home in bed in plenty of time for a school night. How does that sound?"

It sounded wonderful. So ordinary, so... domestic, that was it. It made them sound like a family. Her eyes stung and she took a shaky breath. Could Dodge possibly be right? Was she making things worse by fighting Jeffie's passion?

"Hmm?" Dodge pressed, and bent to kiss the corner of her mouth. He was starting to smile, as if he could sense her wavering.

Was it his words that were swaying her, or his lips? Or was it the spark that had rekindled deep in her chest? He still wanted her company this evening, even with a seven-year-old chaperon in tow. That was a revelation to be treasured, to be examined minutely when she had time and breath to consider it. But now was not the time, not with Dodge's mouth covering hers. His kiss was swift and fierce, an unspoken declaration of his victory in this dispute. As their lips parted, he smiled in unabashed triumph.

"Good," he said crisply. "Okay, let's get cooking."

Funny, she already felt as if she'd been standing over a hot stove all afternoon. With a rueful smile, she let go of his jacket lapels, then her smile faded as her eyes returned to Jeffie. He was removing the black bishop from the game. He swiveled the board again and scowled down at the remaining black warriors.

Dodge slid open the door and preceded her into the cabin. "Hiya, Jeff," he said casually.

The boy turned his head, swept blind eyes across the two of them and returned to his problem. Pocketing her mittens, Coffee clenched her hands until her nails dug into her palms. She'd been wrong—crazy—to let Dodge reassure her.

But she stayed where she was as the grand master crossed the room. He squatted on his heels beside the low table. "Who's winning?" he asked, laying a hand on Jeffie's shoulder.

Jeffie's long, silvery lashes fluttered several times, then his eyes focused on Dodge. "White... But black could win. I could win black, if white didn't know what I was doing." His dazed face came to life as inspiration hit. "Will you play white?"

Coffee could see Dodge's mouth tighten. He wanted to, as much as Jeffie wanted him to. She clasped her hands harder. *Oh, Dodge, can I trust you?*

As if he'd heard that thought, he darted a glance at her, then grimaced and looked back at the child. "Some other time I'd love that, Jeff. But tonight your mom and I thought we'd take you to a movie. So let's go make some supper first, shall we?"

Jeffie didn't even acknowledge the suggestion. "If you play white I'll give you your knights back," he wheedled.

It wasn't going to work. For a moment she'd let herself hope that Dodge had some magical way of curbing this obsession, but—

Dodge laughed. "You'd give back my knights? You've never heard the saying Never Give a Sucker an Even Break?"

"It wouldn't matter," Jeff confided. "I can beat you anyway."

Dodge's amusement faded to a look in which compassion fused with respect. "Wouldn't surprise me, pal. Wouldn't surprise me at all." Reaching out, he took the board and lifted it an inch or two off the table. "But right now...we have to put this away." He waited, the board hovering within the boy's reach. "Okay? I'll save—" He glanced at Coffee, noted her frozen face, and his jaw muscles slowly knotted. "I'll save your positions for you."

He wasn't her ally. She had to remember that. No matter how he made her feel, he was on Jeffie's side. On the side of that dreadful game. She took a shuddering breath and stepped forward, but Jeffie was nodding, giving reluctant permission.

"Okay," he said.

"Good." Dodge whisked the board away and set it on top of a tall bookshelf. "Now..." His voice turned almost hearty with relief. "I think we'll put you in charge of poking up that fire, Jeff. Looks like it's got a few coals left. And your mom and I will scout out the kitchen."

Turning, he reached for Coffee. He caught the zipper on her jacket and started it downward. "See?" he said under his breath. "All it takes is a firm hand."

"Anyway, we don't need the board," Jeffie said, stopping beside them. "It's black's move. I'm gonna move my king to B1. So now it's your move."

"You—" Dodge's hand froze in midair, with Coffee's jacket half-unzipped. "Where'd you learn board notation?"

"That magazine." Jeffie pointed to an open magazine on the couch. "I read about Denisov—Deniv— A game a man with a funny name played with a lady. It told all the moves." His face almost glowing, he smiled up at Dodge. "A *lot* of people play chess, don't they?"

"Yeah..." Dodge's face was a mask as he looked from Jeff to Coffee and back again. "They do."

He moved to finish the task he'd set himself, but Coffee reached out and caught his wrist, stopping the motion. She'd been a fool, a wishful fool, to think this could ever work. As Dodge looked up from her zipper she returned his gaze steadily, her teeth clamping into her lower lip as she fought for the courage to do what she must.

"So where are you gonna move then?" Jeffie tugged at Dodge's sleeve.

The grand master didn't glance down at him. His eyes were burning into Coffee's, sending her a message that might have been a plea, but looked more like an ultimatum. "Rook to Q1," he said, his voice gritty with emotion.

"Knight to Q4!" Jeffie snapped.

"Pawn to..." Still holding her eyes, Dodge let go of her zipper. His lips twitched for a second as she zipped herself up again, but Coffee couldn't have said if it was with regret or concentration as he plotted his next move in the game. "Pawn to KN3," he said evenly, then to Coffee, "Don't go. We're almost done."

She shook her head—there was nothing left to say. Turning, she found Jeffie's coat and put it on him. He lifted his arms for the sleeves in reflex, all his attention centered on Dodge's face. "I wouldn't do that," he warned his opponent.

"No?" A flash of humor warmed Dodge's face, then his expression went blank again. His eyes were still fastened on Coffee as she pulled Jeffie's cap out of his pocket and settled it on his head. "Well, I do a lot of things you wouldn't do, pal," he added absently. "Yet..." He shook his head at Coffee again. "Stay," was all he said, but that one word held a world of emotion.

"Then my knight...uh, knight to B3!" Jeffie sang out.

How could she fight this? They didn't need a board or even pieces to play. Coffee shuddered and put her hands on Jeffie's shoulders, pulling him back against her thighs. She could take her son's body with her, but Dodge had his mind. She wanted to fling herself on the man, beat on his chest and scream at him till her own tears choked her. *You see what you've done?* she stormed at him with her eyes.

But Dodge was crouching on his heels before them. His hands settled on Jeffie's shoulders, covering her fingers with his own. "That's mate in two more moves, Jeff," he said softly. "You're quite a guy. I resign."

"You're not going to finish?" Jeffie protested.

"Nope. That's the way it's done. It's not in the rules, but it's how a gentleman plays," Dodge told him, and rocked him gently on his feet. "When you know you're beat, you resign." His fingers contracted, squeezing Coffee's hands as well as Jeffie's shoulders, then he held out his hand. "Good game, Jeff. Thanks."

She would not cry—couldn't, in front of Jeffie, not that he would have noticed as he grinned, his small fingers enveloped by the man's. She took another breath, then said, her voice almost a croak, "Okay, Jeffums, let's go." She nudged him away from Dodge and toward the door.

He glanced up at her in total surprise. "We're going? What about—"

"We'll see a movie some other time. I think maybe tonight isn't a good night after all."

He let out a little-boy groan of disappointment that sounded so normal tears sprang to her eyes in spite of her resolution. Face averted, she steered him across the room.

"Coffee?" Dodge called behind her, his voice grating. "I'm going to ski again tomorrow. Come with me?"

Without turning, she shook her head and reached for the door latch. "I don't think—" She swallowed a sob.

"The Ellis River Trail, Coffee," he insisted. "After noon. I hope you'll change your mind..." *About everything,* he seemed to be saying.

If she could have...if only were there were some way...

"I'll go!" Jeffie volunteered as she hustled him out onto the deck.

"I'd like that, Jeff," Dodge said, coming to stand in the doorway. "But you'll have to ask you mother."

She shook her head, still avoiding Dodge's eyes. "You can't, Jeffums. You'll be in school. And tomorrow is Anke's day off, so after school I want you to watch Gitta for her."

Jeffie let out another long-suffering groan, and she gave him a gentle push. "Now scoot. Go get your skis on."

With a grimace and a glum, "G'night, Dodge," he trudged down the stairs.

There was nothing left to say, nothing to stay for, and yet she couldn't seem to go. She swung her head an inch or so, and from the corner of her eye could see Dodge's lean form still standing behind her. "You're letting your heat out," she muttered.

She felt more than saw him shrug. "Couldn't get much colder, could it?"

No. Her breath steamed in the darkness, and the cold was clawing into her soul. She shook her head, the hot tears streaming, but whether they were for the evening together that had slipped through their fingers, or for something much larger, much more precious, that had slipped away, she could not have said. "Good night, Dodge," she murmured, and started for the stairs.

"See you later," he called after her, and his voice had lost its bitter edge.

But even though it had... She hunched her shoulders. *Not if I see you first, Dodge Phillips.* From now on, it would hurt too much to look at him.

STAY BUSY. SHE'D USED that rule to fight off sadness before. Sooner or later it would work again. So when Maureen decided to cook supper for the first time since her accident the next day, Coffee skied down to the village to buy her a pound of mozzarella. Not that she felt the least bit hungry for homemade pizza or any other food, but at least the errand would keep her busy.

Coming out of the small gas station and grocery store, Coffee stopped on the porch to tuck the package of cheese into her backpack, then shrug her pack into place. She glanced at the elementary school across the road. Jeffie would be safely occupied there for another two hours, and Dodge... She frowned, then looked up at the sky. The forecast was for snow this afternoon, and lots of it. Surely he'd heard? This was no day to start up the Ellis River Trail alone. She bit her lip as she considered phoning him with the warning, then shook her head. He was a big boy and a very smart one. He didn't need her to take care of him. She reached for the skis that were propped against the outer wall of the store, then stopped as a voice called her name.

"Coffee!" Peter Bradford called again. He was crossing the street from the direction of the Jackson Ski Touring Center. "Is Anke in there?" he asked eagerly, lowering his voice as he tramped over the ridge of plowed snow at the edge of the road.

"Anke?" Coffee shook her head. "I haven't seen her since this morning. It's her day off. She said something about driving down to North Conway."

"Oh..." His shaggy brows knit together. "Well, her car's parked down the street." He nodded back the way he had come. "She's not in the center so I thought..." He shrugged, suddenly looking very sheepish.

Coffee hid her smile. "Maybe the tavern?" She nodded at the Wildcat, though lunch in its dining room would surely be a bit rich for Anke's blood. But perhaps she'd stopped in at the bar. "I'm headed for the post office, so if I see her over there, I'll tell her you're looking for her."

"Thanks...." Clapping her on the shoulder, Peter headed for the tavern.

Coffee looked after his broad figure for a moment, her amusement fading. Any cheer Peter had brought with him he'd taken away again. *He didn't even stop to chat.* With a little hiss of self-annoyance, she squared her shoulders. It was absurd to feel neglected, when she'd never wanted Peter for more than a friend.... If she was lonely, it was not for him.

"Excuse me, miss?" An older woman leaned out the passenger-side window of a car that had stopped before the store. "Could you tell us how to find the Village House?"

"Of course." While Coffee gave the woman and her husband directions, she stole a glance over her shoulder. She was just in time to see Peter leaving the Wildcat with a scowl on his rugged face. Turning away from her, he stalked off in the opposite direction. Coffee frowned. *Strange.* Then she turned back to the tourists.

Once they had driven on, she returned to the porch for her skis. What had made Peter so mad? she wondered as she took hold of them. She looked over her shoulder again, and understood. Now Anke was leaving the tavern. She smiled up at Dodge as he held the door for her, then preceded him down the walk.

Two long strides took Coffee into the shadow of the store doorway. She shoved on inside, then checked her headlong flight. Assuming a casual air, she jammed her hands into her pockets and sauntered over to a bookrack by the window. So...now she knew exactly what Peter had been feeling, she thought as she stared sightlessly at the paperbacks. That sharp little knife twisting somewhere near the heart....

A moment later the black Porsche zipped past the window and Coffee let out a little sigh. He was heading uphill toward his cabin. If she'd agreed to go skiing with him at noon, he would have had two dates in one day. *Quite the busy guy, aren't you, Dodge?* she jeered at him mentally, but it didn't help the sadness, nor the confusion. Last night she would have sworn that he— She shook her head, dislodging that thought. It didn't matter anyway. Wouldn't make the least bit of difference. She took a deep breath. Well, if he was staying busy, then so should she. The post office, then home... then she'd clean the oven. She'd been putting that off for days.

But after she'd picked up the mail, which came to the bed-and-breakfast's post office box, the new clerk called her over. "You'd better give Jeffie a little talking to," he told her with a grin. "He's got the right idea, but he's missing a few refinements." He brought out a torn letter from under the counter, then a box filled with pennies. "Look what he was trying to send through the mail!" he chortled, jingling the pennies. "And with only a twenty-five-cent stamp. The whole thing came apart when he dropped it through the mail slot." He handed her the envelope and grinned again. "Whatever he was trying to buy, he must have wanted it bad. Looks like he cleaned out his piggy bank."

It did indeed, Coffee thought, as she numbly accepted the box of pennies and the envelope. With a word of thanks she turned away, then stopped near the door, reading the printed address on the letter that he must have mailed on his way to school that morning.

It was addressed to the American Chess Federation, in Boston. Blindly she pushed out the door, then stopped again, taking in deep, shaky breaths of the frigid air. But it didn't help. *Oh, God, it's starting.* A fringe of icicles hung from the edge of the post office roof. She felt as if one of them had been driven right through her, a glistening, freezing shaft of pure terror. *Jeffie...* Pulling out the paper that was folded inside his envelope, she scanned it, her teeth buried in her bottom lip.

It was an entry blank, printed on the slick paper magazines were made of, with a ragged edge where it had been ripped out—the chess periodical that Jeffie had been reading last night. Still she shook her head, refusing to believe it. This was an entry blank for a chess tournament, to be held next month in Boston. The pennies were Jeffie's entry fee. She shook her head again. *Jeffie, oh, Jeffie, no...* Lifting her head, she stared toward the schoolhouse as if she could see him through its wall, and actually took a step in that direction. Then she stopped herself.

Taking a deep breath, she shut her eyes for a moment. *Steady.* The terror she was feeling, that was all for the future. For the moment he was still safe, sitting in his little desk behind those walls. And he would come safely home to her, once school was done. She'd insisted he ride the school bus this morning, using the coming snow as her excuse to keep him off his skis. That way there'd be no stopping by Dodge's on his way home.

Not for Jeffie, anyway. Carefully folding the letter, she tucked it and the pennies into her pack. But as for her...she'd be skiing past Dodge's cabin on her way home. And it was time they talked. This was the final straw. *If you'd only just left us alone, Dodge Phillips.* Well, he would. If it was the last thing she did in this world, she'd make sure that he left them alone after today.

For once skiing up from the valley did nothing to calm her. Each rasping stroke of ski through the snow seemed to rip at her heart. And the smoke she saw rising from his chimney to the darkening sky as she skied up through the little pines might have been the smoke of burning dreams. But it didn't matter. She wouldn't *let* it matter. All that should matter was Jeffie.

As she crossed the deck, she saw that Dodge was working at his computer. His eyes fixed on the lit screen, he didn't hear her boots on the boards. Clenching her teeth—she'd seen such concentration before—she rapped on the glass, then slid open the door when he swung around.

His face lit with pleasure as he got to his feet. "I'm glad you changed your mind, Coffee, but haven't you heard the forecast?"

Why couldn't he act like what he was—her enemy? That would have been so much easier to take than this warm smile, which was now fading as he studied her face. "I didn't come to go skiing." She took a half step backward to avoid his hand, which was reaching for her shoulder. "I came to ask you to go. Get out of town. You've got to."

He stood motionless for a moment, then his dark brows drew together. "Why? Because of last night?"

"Because of that, and because of this." She yanked off her backpack, snatched the letter out of its pocket and thrust it at him. "Did you put him up to this? Tell him you'd take him?" Her voice was raw with unshed tears. Hugging herself hard to contain them, she wheeled away as he read the entry blank, then swung back again in time to see his lips curl in the ghost of a grin.

He looked up and his face was solemn again. "I knew nothing about this, Coffee, believe me. But—"

Anger didn't replace grief, it combined with it in a lacerating emotion that tore at her throat. "But *nothing,* Dodge Phillips! This was what I've been afraid of since the minute you set foot in this town. You're ruining everything! Now will you please, please, *please* get out of our lives, and let me start picking up the pieces?"

As her voice cracked, his hands lifted, then dropped again to his sides. His long fingers tensed against his thighs. "I told you, Coffee—not till I get the answer to one last question," he said heavily.

The reason Richard quit chess—that had become the prize in their game, hadn't it? And chess players never quit playing while there was something left to win; she should know. Whirling away from him, she dug her fingers into her forearms until she winced, but the pain cleared her head for a moment. Well, she defined winning another way. Winning to her was Jeffie safe and sane and free from the dark obsession this man had brought with him. She would settle for that.

And when his book comes out? a small interior voice reminded her. She bit her lip. That would not be for a year or two. And with any luck, Jeffie might not see it for several years after that. She would trade future worries for present security if she had to. What mattered right now was that, with Dodge in his life, Jeffie was going to grow more and more obsessed with chess, until she couldn't reach him anymore, any more than she'd been able to reach Richard. What mattered was driving Dodge out of their lives before that happened.

"All right..." she said, her voice shaking. "You like to make trades, Dodge. Here's a trade for you. I'll answer your question as best I can, why Richard quit chess... and you take the answer and go. Is that a deal?"

Two long strides closed the distance between them, and he caught her arms. "That's what you want?" he demanded, his eyes boring into her. "You really want me to go, Coffee?"

His fingers were hurting her, though the pain was nothing compared to the pain inside as she met his eyes squarely. But she'd trade her pain for Jeffie's happiness any day. That was just the way it was. "Yes!" she whispered, her voice choked with tears.

He didn't let her go so much as shove her from him, then he swung away. "Okay..." He walked over to the stove, dropped down on his heels and opened its glass door. "So tell me," he said bitterly, and shut the door without adding another log.

All the nervous energy had drained out of her with the victory, if that's what it was. It didn't feel like one. "Okay..." She sank down on the couch and stared at the floor. "But I'm asking you one more thing...."

His contemptuous snort told her that she'd already made her deal and could now live with it.

"For Jeffie's sake," she said stubbornly. "I don't want you to put this in your book. I'm *begging* you. You'll see why, once I've told you." And so, without looking up from the floor, she told him, her words stumbling and painful as she described the months after Richard had come home victorious from the world championship. His confusion, his bitterness, his final words as he walked out the door. "It's chess that did that to him, Dodge. That's why I hate it so."

Tears drowning her eyes, she looked up blindly. "Chess robbed him of *everything*. He sacrificed everything else in his life for one single-minded purpose—to be the best in the world. And once he'd become that...he—he didn't have any purpose left.... That's what he was struggling against, those last eight months...and finally...he just gave up."

Dodge sank down on his heels before her and caught her clasped hands. "Let me get this straight. You think he skied up the mountain and just let himself freeze?" He laughed, a harsh, protesting sound. "Coffee, that's crazy! He must have slipped, hurt an ankle or hit his head. Anything could have happened up there. You can't think—"

"I don't think—I know." And so she told him about the letter that Maureen had found in Richard's desk, the fourth day he was missing, after they'd given up hope. Closing her eyes for a moment, she could see the scene just the way it had happened. She'd walked into Richard's study, to surprise Maureen standing by his old rolltop desk, reading a sheet of paper covered with his nervous scrawl. Once again she could see the stricken look in Maureen's eyes, hear the driven snow lashing against the windows and the freight-train moan of the wind as it swept down the mountain.

"He left a suicide note?" Dodge's expression was utterly stupefied when she opened her eyes. "What did it say?"

"I didn't read it." When his eyebrows shot up she added, "Maureen wouldn't let me. She said it would only hurt me." Knowing Richard's talent for blaming others, for using words to wound, and seeing the look of pain on Maureen's face, Coffee had believed her. "I hurt enough already, Dodge, knowing he was dead...knowing I could have stopped him.... If Maureen said that letter would only hurt me more, I believed her. I didn't *want* any more...I couldn't have taken it.... So I didn't..."

Dodge settled onto the couch beside her. Warm hands slid beneath her thighs and behind her back, and he lifted her into his lap. "You poor kid...." Pulling her against his chest, he settled his cheek on her head. "And you've been blaming yourself ever since, huh?" He brushed his lips across her temple. "Where's that letter now?"

Her moment of wondrous comfort vanished. He might be holding her like a lover, but he was thinking like a biographer. Utterly defeated, she rested her forehead against his shoulder. "Don't know," she said dully. "I guess Maureen destroyed it."

"I...see...." There was a note of vibrant energy in those two words, almost of gaiety.

She sighed, then breathed in his warm, wonderful scent as she inhaled again. So now he was happy. He had the pieces to his puzzle. And she...she had his word. "So...that's why I hate chess, for what it did to Richard," she murmured against his shirt. "That's why I'll never let

Jeffie get involved with it.... That's why I want you to leave.''

Pressed as close as she was against him, she felt his start of surprise. Raising her head, she met his dark eyes. "You *are* leaving..." she reminded him. "That was the deal. You said you would.''

"Yes, but—"

She shook her head fiercely. "No buts about it, Dodge! I'd never have told you if you hadn't agreed!''

His face had gone blank. She could almost hear the wheels spinning behind that mask, then he glanced toward the windows. "Okay, I agreed, but I didn't say when. You want me to pack up and go in the middle of a blizzard?"

Turning in his arms, she discovered it was snowing. She shuddered. "No...but tomorrow?"

The masklike stillness broke for a second into an expression that was almost painfully vulnerable, then it hardened. "If you want me to...but you'll have to ask me again tomorrow.''

Before she could protest that that was unfair, he'd kissed her, a swift, businesslike kiss, and swung her off his lap. "Okay, let's get moving. I've got an errand to run before this gets any worse.''

He insisted on driving her up the hill to the inn, though she would rather have skied. As they swung into the parking lot, he scanned the cars. "Looks like you've got a guest or two. But where's Anke's car?"

"If it's not here, she's not back yet.''

He drummed his fingers on the steering wheel. "Do you know where she was planning to shop in North Conway?"

He was asking her? He'd talked to Anke more recently than she had. But Coffee was past hurting. She'd reached a state of numbness that she hoped would last for a long, long time. "No." She shrugged tiredly and slipped out of the car.

A moment later she was standing skis in hand, the warmth of his kiss fading from her cheek, watching the black car swoop across the bridge and down the hill at a breakneck pace. But she was too numb to wonder anymore.

In the family room, Maureen sat in her chair near the fire, her lap filled with bright quilt patches while Gitta played at her feet. She looked up with a smile, then put down her needle. "What's wrong?"

I've sent away the only man I might have loved. She couldn't say it. Maureen would find out for herself soon enough. Coffee shrugged and shook her head. "Headache. I'm going to make some tea. Would you like a cup?"

Maureen's narrowed eyes didn't buy that excuse, but she had a Yankee's respect for emotional privacy. "That'd be nice."

Coffee glanced at the mantel clock. "Is Jeffie back?"

"Not yet."

The school bus would be creeping along in this weather, Coffee told herself as she headed for the kitchen. But a moment later she heard the front door close with a bang, then Jeffie's scampering feet. "In here, Jeffums!" she called, and put the water on to boil.

"Wow! It's *snowing!*" Pink-cheeked with the cold, he bounced into the room, trailing his wool scarf behind him. He dropped it as she stooped to hug him. "Can I go play with Dodge?"

Which was he going to miss more, she wondered, the question wrenching at her heart. Chess or the man who'd opened that door for him? "Not today, big boy, you're the designated baby-sitter, remember?" She didn't yet have the heart to tell him that Dodge was leaving. When he let out an aggrieved moan, she only smiled. "Want some hot chocolate before you get to work?"

While she made his chocolate, he sat at the table and told her about his day. She answered absently, her mind on her own worry. What should she say about his letter? She'd thought at first that she would ignore the incident, but that would leave Jeffie waiting forever for a response that would never come. Or worse yet, the postman would tease him about the pennies, and he'd learn in that way that she'd intercepted his entry. No, it was better to face up to it.

Crossing to the backpack that she'd hung on a hook near the back door, she took out the envelope. "Jeffums, the postman gave me this." As she explained, she watched his expression change until she was facing a softer, rounder version of Dodge's poker face. He was shutting her out, watching her with a wary stoicism that chilled her to the bone.

So he hadn't forgotten to mention the letter this morning. As she'd feared, he'd meant it to be a secret. Before Dodge, they'd never kept secrets from each other. "It wasn't a good idea, anyway, Jeffums," she finished gently. "Boston's too far away. I couldn't have driven you down there. We've got Gram to take care of, and the guests."

"Dodge will take me," Jeffie said stubbornly. "He likes chess."

Sooner or later she was going to have to tell him. There was no way she could spare him the news, or the pain that would come with it. It might as well be now. She smoothed the bangs off his forehead. "Dodge can't take you, darling. He's going away."

A slap would have gained her the same reaction. His little body jerked with the words, then his eyes widened in shock. "He's—" He shook his head, flatly rejecting the news. "He can't. He *can't!*"

"I'm afraid he's got to, big boy. He was just here for a visit, like one of our guests. People come and go...."

But not Dodge, Jeffie's wounded eyes protested.

Not Dodge, her own treacherous heart agreed. She reached for Jeffie, and the kettle on the stove whistled. "Hang on, baby...." She touched his cheek, then went to shut off the steam-driven wail. But when she turned back again, Jeffie was gone.

Into the family room, she decided, looking down the empty hall. She started after him, then checked herself. If she crowded him now with her sympathy, he'd only reject her, maybe even blame her for Dodge's going. It would be better to give him a minute to absorb the blow and then try to sooth him. In the meantime, Gitta's uncomplicated gaiety might be the best distraction of all. And he often turned to Maureen for comfort. She would leave him to their attentions while she put the tea tray together.

But minutes later, when she carried the tray into the room, she found only Maureen and Gitta awaiting her. "Jeffie didn't come in?" she asked in surprise.

Maureen looked up from her patchwork. "Didn't know he was home yet."

Upstairs in his bedroom then, Coffee decided with an absent nod. So he was taking it even worse than she'd feared, she thought as she poured out Maureen's tea. She settled Gitta down to a snack of cookies and milk, then left them to it. Hurrying toward the stairs, she stopped in dismay as the front door opened and a smiling young couple barged in, their arms full of skis and baggage.

"Ms. Dugan?" the man asked, dropping his gear and advancing on her with outstretched hand. "I'm Eric Lundgren. We have reservations for six for this weekend, remember? But we saw the forecast this morning and decided it was come now or be snowed out, so we jumped in our cars and here we are." As if to dramatize his words, another beaming couple trooped through the door, brushing snow off their shoulders. "We were hoping you could take us early, and I see your vacancy sign's out." He gave her an engaging grin.

"Yes...of course...." Coffee would have been just as happy to bundle them back out the door and lock it behind them, but that wasn't the way to stay in business. Forcing a smile to her face, she moved to the front desk and reached for the registry.

It took almost an hour to settle the guests in and make their tea. As soon as she could, Coffee hurried up the stairs to Jeffie's room. "Jeffums?" When he didn't answer her knock, she pushed open his door, then sucked in her breath. The room was as neat and untouched as she'd left it this morning, when she'd changed his bedclothes. Clearly he'd not been there since. "Jeffums?" She covered the other bedrooms on the third floor with mounting dread, then rattled down the stairs to the second floor and peeked into Anke's room. But he wasn't there. "Jeffie," she whispered, staring out the window at the falling snow. Then he would be in the family room, or the kitchen.

But she took the stairs to the first floor two at a time. The front door opened as she descended the last step, and she almost vaulted into Dodge's arms.

"What's the matter?" he demanded, holding on to her when she would have backed away. Behind him, Anke stood in the doorway, her face white and her eyes wide with alarm.

"Jeffie," Coffee said. Twisting out of his arms, she almost ran to the family room, looked inside and backed out again. He wasn't there. *Be in the kitchen,* she told him. But he was not.

Dodge caught up with her in the sunroom, where she stood staring down into the mudroom. "Coffee!" His hands clamped on her arms. "Tell me."

"Jeffie . . . he must have skied down to your place." With an effort she wrenched her eyes from the wall where his skis should have been propped. "Did you lock the cabin?" But even as she asked she remembered his hand moving against the latch, the soft click as he locked it.

Dodge's eyes shared the memory. "Let's go!" He caught her arm as she started for her skis. "By car, Coffee. The roads are still passable."

"But I'm taking my skis." And she prayed she would not need them.

CHAPTER ELEVEN

OUTSIDE DODGE'S CABIN, Coffee almost danced with impatience while he unlocked the door nearest the driveway. His skis were propped beside it—she sent one toppling into the snow, then picked it up again. "What are these doing here?" she demanded, simply to be talking.

"I practiced this morning—skied up the road." Dodge pushed through the door and she followed on his heels.

But Jeffie wasn't waiting for them. Out on the deck, a trampled path paralleling the glass showed where he had marched back and forth to stay warm. It was only half filled in with fresh snow. Leaning over the railing, she could still make out his tracks, cutting back down the mountain. "He's headed home," she said and whirled around. He had to be. "I'm going after him."

"Then you've got company." But Dodge caught her as she started back to the Porsche for her skis. "First tell somebody where we're going—Maureen or your friend Bradford. I'll throw on another layer."

He was thinking straighter than she was, she realized, as she dialed Peter's number with shaking fingers. All she could think of was Jeffie's wounded eyes . . . and her child's headlong stubbornness. He'd gone running to Dodge; would he turn back before he'd found him? And if not, where would he seek him? If he had looked for Dodge's skis below the deck, the only place Jeffie had ever seen skis stored at Dodge's cabin, and found them gone . . . Could he have jumped to the conclusion— *Oh, please God, no.* Peter's answering machine came on and she took a sobbing breath. "Peter, this is Coffee, at four-thirty. There's a chance that Jeffie's heading up the Ellis River Trail. If I don't report in by five, that's where I'm bound. Dodge is with me. Thanks."

She turned to find Dodge behind her. "You think he went looking for me?" he demanded.

"Yesterday you said you'd be skiing there."

"But damn it, Coffee, my car was gone. Wouldn't he realize—"

"He didn't check. His tracks don't lead around the front of the house." It didn't surprise her. In Jeffie's world, skis were the primary means of transportation. And he'd been upset, perhaps already befuddled by the cold.

"Then let's go." Catching her hand, Dodge hustled her out of the cabin.

All the way downhill to the intersection with the main trail, Coffee prayed. *Let him turn uphill. Please God, let him turn.*

But the faint grooves that were all that remained of his tracks turned downhill. Coffee shook her head, then kept on shaking it, denying the evidence. *First Richard, and now Jeffie.* No, it couldn't happen twice; she wouldn't permit it. Could not bear it.

Dodge caught her around the shoulders and gave her a shake. "How much of a head start has he got?" he demanded, his mouth at her ear. The wind was growing gustier, each distinct blast rolling relentlessly down the mountains with the rising wail of a freight train.

"An hour?" Maybe less if he'd waited long at the cabin.

Dodge nodded and his arm tightened in an encouraging hug. "We're not going to lose him, Coffee." He kissed her face, his lips hot on her cheek. "I promise you we're not.

But let's not lose each other, okay?'' He kissed her again. "Stay close." Letting her go, he started down the trail in a crouching snowplow.

The Ellis River Trail...in how many dreams had she skied that remorselessly rising path with the black river rushing beside it? How many times in her sleep had she followed Richard's tracks up that white tunnel through the dark, overhanging trees, pleading, *no, it's not over?*

Not over, her skis sang through the deepening snow. Not over, Dodge had promised her. But still Jeffie's slogging tracks led north toward Mount Washington, until the drifting white wiped them out.

Gliding in a dream, half-stunned by the flying snow and the cold, Coffee followed by faith alone now. But who was Jeffie following? The father who had passed this way three winters before, or the man who now matched her stride for stride?

Dodge caught her arm to stop her. "Breathe a minute," he panted in her ear.

"Only a minute," she agreed reluctantly, though with another blast approaching, he probably couldn't hear her. Pressing as close together as they could, wearing skis, they shared body heat and something even more precious.

Dodge turned her face into his shoulder as the gust arrived. Once the worst had swept past them, he pushed up the rim of her cap and put his lips to her ear. "Is there any way off this trail?"

Bounded on the right by the river, the trail was hemmed in by a wall of mountains to the left. That was the way Richard had gone. A few miles north of where they stood, he'd turned off the trail to start his climb toward the timberline. But Jeffie...if it really was Dodge Jeffie was following, he'd stick to the trail. "No," she shouted back.

"Then we'll find him," Dodge promised. "We'll find him soon."

Without Dodge, she would have missed him. A quarter-mile up the trail, the grand master stopped her. Downed years ago in some winter storm, a massive white birch lay alongside the path. With its trunk split some three feet above the snow, the shattered butt was still propped atop the remaining stump. The rude triangular shelter thus created protected the ground directly beneath, and the drifts to either side had formed a tiny snow cave. Dodge pointed to the pair of skis propped up against the trunk. They were already so frosted with snow she had looked right past them.

"Jeffie!" Coffee kicked out of her bindings and waded through the drifts, with Dodge tramping on her heels. "Jeffums!"

Sheltered from the wind in the bare spot beneath the overhanging trunk, Jeffie had curled up like a small, hibernating animal. He'd pulled the drawstring on his parka hood so tight that only his mouth was visible when Dodge scooped him up. His smile was sleepy as they hugged him between them. "Knew you'd come," he murmured, then burrowed his face into Dodge's shoulder.

"Glad somebody wasn't worried!" Dodge laughed at Coffee over the child's head. "Now what's the fastest way out of here? Back the way we came?"

Coffee nodded. It was, though with the snow getting deeper every minute, it was going to be slow going, carrying Jeffie. But she didn't doubt for a minute that they would do it. Tonight, between them, she and Dodge could do anything.

Then her head swung around as she realized the distant roar she heard was not the next gust of wind. With a little laugh, she caught Dodge's arm and urged him toward the trail. Their luck was running straight and true tonight, as unbreakable as the thread of emotion that stretched tight between them.

The rider of the lead snowmobile that came roaring up the trail wore a familiar yellow parka. Lifting an arm, she flagged down Peter Bradford, then hooked her other hand through Dodge's elbow. "To heck with skiing. Let's go home in a cab."

UP ON THE THIRD FLOOR, in Jeffie's bedroom, Coffee could hear the high-spirited babble of the party that had been going on since their return. Peter and his snowmobile buddies, all the guests of the Owl Brook Inn, and Maureen and Anke were banishing their earlier fears in a rollicking celebration down in the guest lounge. With a smile, Coffee brushed the damp bangs off Jeffie's forehead. She had popped him straight into a warm bath on their return, and now he was tucked in under a mound of blankets. And that was where he was staying, safe and sound for the rest of the night, even though he'd begun to perk up again.

"Where's Dodge?" Jeffie mumbled.

"Right here."

Coffee turned to find the grand master standing in the doorway with a tray in his hands. A faint smile quirking his lips, he set the tray on the bedside table. "Ready for some chocolate, Jeff?" When the boy nodded and pushed himself up against the headboard, Dodge handed him a mug. Sitting on the opposite edge of the bed from Coffee, he stretched across to hand her a glass of golden liquor.

"What's that?" Jeffie demanded, his freshly scrubbed face already sporting a chocolate mustache.

"Brandy." Dodge lifted his glass, his eyes holding Coffee's. "And here's the toast—to Jeff, who still has ten fingers and ten toes."

"Not funny," Coffee growled as she took a sip, but Jeffie giggled.

"Can I have some?" With a child's unerring instinct, he directed his appeal to Dodge.

The grand master laughed under his breath and shook his head. "This is for rescuers. You're a rescuee, chum. In the doghouse. You scared us out of a year's growth."

Jeffie digested this in silence, his solemn face half-hidden as he sipped from his mug. "But you scared me," he pointed out finally. "Mommy said you were going."

"I know...." Dodge pulled the blanket that had slipped off Jeffie's legs back into place, then his hand lingered on the boy's knee. "But she was wrong. I'm not going anywhere." He swung to face Coffee. "I'm not," he repeated quietly, but his eyes held a challenge.

Her own eyes began to sting, but she could not look away. Nothing had changed—she still hated and feared chess. And everything had changed. She loved this man—loved his strength, his cleverness, that faint ever-ready curve of his lips and the hunger in his eyes when he looked at her.

And her son loved him, too. "Good," Jeffie proclaimed with sleepy satisfaction. "You better not."

"Not on your sweet life." Dodge rescued the mug from his hands as it began to tilt, then set it aside. His eyes darkening with expectation, he turned back to Coffee as she came around the foot of the bed.

"Good," said Jeffie again, then added, "Mommy says I don't have to go to school tomorrow, so will you come over and play chess?"

Watching her face, Dodge winced, then he stood. "If I can," he promised, and leaned down to kiss Jeffie's forehead. Patting his shoulder, he straightened again. "I will if I can, Jeff. Meantime, may I borrow your mother?" When Jeffie giggled and nodded his permission, Dodge draped an arm over Coffee's shoulders and started her toward the door.

This was how she wanted to walk for the rest of her life, with Dodge's arm around her. But how could she?

At the far end of the hall from Jeffie's room, Dodge turned her to face him, his eyebrows rising in rueful inquiry. With a little sigh of despair, Coffee stepped into his arms. He didn't kiss her at first, he simply caught her to him and held her so tightly it took her breath away. Closing her eyes, she could feel their hearts beat together, an entwined, exultant rhythm that she wished could go on forever.

Putting her lips to his throat, she kissed him—kissed him again as the taste of his skin almost overwhelmed her, then stiffened her body to tell him that he must let her go. When he shook his head and kept on holding her, she felt the tears start again. "You promised..." she reminded him. "You said you'd go."

"Mmm," he agreed, and nuzzled her temple. "And I don't break promises lightly, Coffee, but I'm breaking this one."

It was what she wanted to hear—dreaded to hear. "Why?" she asked, and couldn't help smoothing her hands up his spine.

He tipped his head back so he could see her face. "Because I want to be part of your life," he said simply, "and I want you to be part of mine."

Her eyes overflowed and she hid her face against his throat. "Dodge, if it were just me..." She shook her head hopelessly.

"But it's not." Lacing his fingers into her hair, he tugged her head gently backward till she had to look at him. "It's not just you, and I'm glad of that. He's a terrific kid. I'd love him if he didn't know his rooks from his elbows."

"But he does."

"Does he ever," Dodge agreed, and eased his hold on her hair. Rocking her gently to and fro in his arms, he sighed. "And so do I, Coffee. It's in my blood. I couldn't give it up, and Jeff wouldn't let me give it up if I wanted to."

"I kn-know . . . And that's why—"

"That's why I want you to talk to someone," Dodge cut in decisively. "You think Richard killed himself because of chess, and you think somehow you should have saved him. I say it's time you stopped blaming chess and stopped blaming yourself. So come downstairs. . . ." He turned her toward the stairway.

Wiping her cheeks, she stared up at him. "What are you talking about?"

"You'll see. I'll come back up and sit with Jeff in a second." Without another word, he guided her down to the second floor, then back to the bedroom that was now Anke's. He rapped on the closed door, then smiled at the German when she opened it. "Anke . . ."

Coffee found herself being propelled into the room as Anke retreated before her. She heard Dodge shut the door behind her, and then they were alone. Her eyes moved from the blonde's strained face to the twin bed in the corner where Gitta was curled up and sweetly sleeping, then back.

"She will not wake," Anke assured her, and beckoned her to the opposite end of the room, where two easy chairs faced each other near the window. "Please to sit, Coffee." Anke picked up an envelope off her bureau and held it, her face troubled. "I did not want to hurt you," she said softly. "That is not why I came, that you must believe." She sat down abruptly, placed the letter on her knees and spread her fingers on it. "But Dodge tells me that you hurt already. And this I see for myself. And he says that perhaps I can stop the hurting. . . ."

How? Coffee wanted to cry, but somewhere deep inside, she felt the barest thread of light creep toward her confusion, as if a door were slowly opening on a darkened room.

"This is hard...." Anke whispered. "You will hate me...."

That was the one thing of which Coffee felt sure. She shook her head.

Anke's smile was very sad. "So you think, but..." Squaring her shoulders, she leaned forward and set the letter in Coffee's lap. "This you must read."

The letter was addressed to Anke Meier, at an address in Cologne, Germany. The spidery script was one Coffee had seen a thousand times before. It was Maureen's writing.

The room was so still Coffee could hear the blood surging in her ears, then a soft sleeping murmur from Anke's child. She stared from the letter to Anke's resolute face and back again, then slowly pulled out two folded sheets of paper.

"Yes, that is the one to read first," Anke agreed as she unfolded one sheet. The spare, unembellished script might have been Maureen's own voice, dry to the point of harshness, all its pain and warmth hidden behind the business-like words.

My dear Miss Meier,
I regret to inform you that my son, Richard Dugan, is dead. Enclosed you will find a newspaper clipping to that effect.

I also regret to inform you of a fact that my son should have told you himself. Richard was married, and leaves a wife and a child in my care.

In your letter, which I found in his desk this morning and which I return to you, you ask to borrow some money for complications of your pregnancy...

With a sharp little intake of breath, Coffee looked up. Yes, of course; she should have known. Her face very pink, Anke met her eyes levelly. Coffee swung to stare at the white-blond head on the pillow across the room, and her eyes filled. Richard's child, yes. How had she not known? Jeffie had known instinctively, hadn't he? She looked down again at the letter.

> Enclosed you will find a check. Please consider it a gift, not a loan, and please do me the favor of neither thanking nor contacting me again.
>
> Enclosed also you will find a letter from my son that he had not finished before his death. Though I do not approve of its sentiments, of course I honor his intention by passing it on to you.
>
> And now I can only wish you and your baby the best of luck, my dear, and my sincerest regrets.
>
> Yours truly,
> Maureen Dugan

Slowly, Coffee folded the letter. Yes, she should have known.... Richard's restlessness, his depression and irritability when he'd come back from Berlin—this explained it. He'd not been angry at her, he'd been angry at himself.

"I am so sorry," Anke said softly. "I did not know. I was working in the bar, at the hotel where the American chess players lived. He seemed so...so smart and strong." Her smile was bittersweet. "And I thought he loved me very much."

Remembering her own courtship, Coffee could almost second that rueful smile. Richard, yes, when he'd wanted something...someone... Or perhaps, she told herself, studying the blonde's wistful face, perhaps this time he had really loved; who was she to say?

"And now," Anke said, "the other letter, the one from Richard. Dodge tells me that you think Richard killed himself. This is not so. You must read—"

"I can't." Coffee shook her head. "I can't, Anke. But tell me...." Deep inside, she could feel the door swinging wider, light and hope sweeping in to meet three years of darkness.

"Ah..." Anke looked toward the bed and her child, her eyes glistening, then turned back to Coffee. "He said that he had been thinking, thinking, thinking since he left me, and that now he had decided he should not have gone. He told about you, and..." She hesitated. "He said that he cared for you, very much, but it was not love... that you married when you were children and did not know..."

It should have hurt, but it did not. He'd been right; she hadn't known what love was, not as she knew it now.

"He said that he would come to me, but first he must find how to tell you, and that would take more thinking."

And to think, Richard had always gone to the mountains.

"He said that it was time to start a new life. That he had had one life with you and with chess, and that now a new door was opening...." Anke continued.

And inside Coffee, the door had swung wide. In a moment, she would rise and walk through it.

"Then he said that he was going to ski in the mountains, and think, and when he came back he would know how to tell you. And he said that, if you climb high enough, from the tops of the White Mountains you can see the sea on a very clear day. And he said that if the weather was fine, perhaps he would climb that high. He would look at the sea, and think of me and his baby on the other side of it.... And there the letter ends," Anke finished softly.

Tears were streaming down both their faces. Coffee nodded and wiped her cheeks. So Richard had not died in sadness and despair, he'd died in hope, on a fine day above the timberline, looking for the sea. He'd died loving someone. Could anyone ask for more?

She stood and brushed at her eyes. *And he hadn't died for chess*—it was starting to hit her. And that meant—that meant she and Dodge—With a little laugh, Coffee flung her arms wide and hugged Anke. "Oh, Anke...I—thank you!" Holding her off by her arms, she laughed through her flowing tears. "You are so brave to tell me, and I am so sorry, and I—I—*thank* you."

"Then you are not angry?" Anke smiled timidly. "It is all right?"

"Anke, it is *so* all right...." Coffee shook her head, searching for words. "I mean I'm sad, but I'm also...happy. I can let go." *I can go on.* And there was someone waiting for her. She could walk through that door out into blessed sunlight, and Dodge would be waiting for her. "Thank you!" With a radiant smile, Coffee whirled away from the blonde toward the door, then checked herself as she passed the bed. Swooping down, she laid a swift kiss on Gitta's soft cheek, turned back to beam at Anke again, then swung out the door, almost running. There was so much to say. She'd wasted so much time.

But at the foot of the stairs she lost another minute as she ran smack into Peter Bradford.

"Whoa, where's the fire?" he laughed, catching her arms to steady her. "Have you seen—" He stopped and stared. "Hey, what's the matter?"

"Not a thing in the world!" Coffee almost sang. "Anke and I have just been having a good cry. You should try it some time, Peter."

The ski patrolman grinned and shook his head at the mysteries of women. "I'm gonna cry if I can't get Anke to come down and join the party. Do you think she knows how to jitterbug?''

''If she doesn't, you'd better get busy and teach her.'' Coffee patted his shoulder, then pointed behind her. ''She's in the back bedroom.'' She slipped by him, then turned again. ''And Peter?'' she called, walking backward. ''You don't have to worry about Dodge Phillips. That man's going to be out of circulation very, very shortly.''

''Oh, yeah?'' Peter gave her a thumbs up, then laughed as she spun around and rattled up the stairs.

''He is, huh?'' Dodge asked as she reached the landing, to find him standing there.

For just a second her smile wavered, then it widened to reach her eyes. ''You better believe he is!'' she laughed as she swept him into a bear hug.

''And the sooner the better,'' Dodge said with intense satisfaction as his lips sought her face. ''The sooner the better.''

EPILOGUE

WHEN COFFEE PHILLIPS stepped through the door into the family room, Jeffie and her husband were playing in front of the fire. The chessboard on the rug between them was the traveling set that Dodge had given Jeffie for Christmas that year, one that Jeffie carried with him wherever he went. Across the board, man and child faced each other. Their poses mirrored each other exactly—legs crossed Indian fashion, hands on knees, her son's white-blond head and her husband's dark one bent over to study the game. But if their positions were identical, their attitudes were not. Dodge sat with the lithe, loose-jointed ease of a big cat. Jeffie sat with a furious, forward-leaning immobility, as if he were about to dive into the game. His attention was directed at the board like a blaze of light.

Though he was facing his mother, he never looked up. But Dodge's head swung around, and their eyes met and held as they always did when one of them entered a room.

"Maureen says supper in five minutes," Coffee warned him, coming to sit in the easy chair at his back. Though it had been completed almost a year ago, they had received the advance copies of Dodge's book in the mail only that day. To celebrate the event, Maureen and Anke and Peter had invited them up the hill to the Owl Brook Inn for a special supper.

"No problem, I'll be mincemeat by then," Dodge assured her, leaning back against her shins. Catching the hand she rested on his shoulder, he laid a kiss in its palm, then turned back with a groan as Jeffie moved a bishop across the board.

"Check!" Jeffie murmured.

As Dodge let her go and leaned forward to make his next move, Coffee reached for the copy of the biography that lay on the lamp table beside her. Though she'd read the manuscript last spring before Dodge submitted it, she'd not had a chance to more than glance at the finished book since her return from her doctor's appointment in North Conway this afternoon.

Her hands tightened on the closed book for a moment and she smiled to herself, laughter shimmering deep inside. Today was indeed a banner day. She had her own news for Dodge, her own creation to brag about, but she didn't mean to steal his thunder. She'd save that secret for tonight, tell him when they were alone together in bed....

"Check," Jeffie said as he moved again.

Coffee opened the book and looked down at the photographic plate that faced page one. It was a copy of the photo from Maureen's scrapbook. A ten-year-old Richard, dwarfed by his trophy, looked back at her, unsmiling. Her eyes misting, she reached out to stroke a finger across his cheek, with fondness but without regret. He'd played some chess games that would be remembered a hundred years from now, and he'd left two wonderful children to do his smiling for him. It was no mean legacy.

Flipping through the book, she came to a plate on the very last page that she had missed in her earlier inspection. It was a photo of Jeffie, taken at his first tournament, last spring. Clutching his second-place trophy, he had a wide, blissful grin on his face. He'd been looking, she remembered, straight past the photographer at her and Dodge when it was taken.

Her eyes filled again—this was Dodge's own private message to her, wasn't it? His promise that joy lay ahead for them all. *Oh, I love you, I do!* Swooping forward, she leaned over his shoulder to kiss his cheek.

"Mmm." He smiled abstractedly, reached up to catch the nape of her neck and keep her there, then laid his king over on its side. "I give," he told Jeffie. Releasing her, he held out his hand. "You had me on the run, Jeff."

Glee and love struggled in her son's face as they shook hands. "Yeah," he agreed. "But... but it's just a game." Embarrassed, he glanced toward the hall and spotted Gitta standing in the doorway, her thumb in her rosebud mouth. *"Hooo!"* he moaned, reverting instantly from chess prodigy to small, mischievous boy. "Haw!" He raised his arms and curled his hands into claws. With great stomping monster steps, he chased his giggling sister from the room.

"Easy for him to say!" Dodge muttered, collecting the chess pieces. "The best I've done this week is a draw. He just gets better and better."

Settling on the rug beside him, Coffee picked up the black king. "We've got about a minute left till supper. You can play me, if you'd like a quick win."

Taking the king from her fingers, Dodge feathered it across her lips. "Could we postpone that till after?" he proposed, his voice growing huskier. "With you I'd rather... prolong the game."

Holding his eyes, Coffee's smile was a promise. "Check, mate," she said lightly.

They laughed, then both turned as Jeffie swung around the doorjamb, one-handed. "Mommy? Dad? Gram says to tell you supper's on the table."

"We're on our way," Dodge assured him, getting to his feet, then lifting Coffee to hers. Hand in hand, they followed him out the door.

my VALENTINE 1992

Celebrate the most romantic day of the year with
MY VALENTINE 1992—a sexy new collection of four
romantic stories written by our famous Temptation
authors:

> **GINA WILKENS**
> **KRISTINE ROLOFSON**
> **JOANN ROSS**
> **VICKI LEWIS THOMPSON**

My Valentine 1992—an exquisite escape into a romantic
and sensuous world.

 Harlequin Books®

VAL-92

HARLEQUIN
PROUDLY PRESENTS
A DAZZLING NEW CONCEPT IN ROMANCE FICTION

One small town—twelve terrific love stories

Welcome to Tyler, Wisconsin—a town full of people
you'll enjoy getting to know, memorable friends and
unforgettable lovers, and a long-buried secret that
lurks beneath its serene surface....

JOIN US FOR A YEAR IN THE LIFE OF TYLER

Each book set in Tyler is a self-contained love story;
together, the twelve novels stitch the fabric of a
community.

LOSE YOUR HEART TO TYLER!

The excitement begins in March 1992, with
WHIRLWIND, by Nancy Martin. When lively, brash
Liza Baron arrives home unexpectedly, she moves
into the old family lodge, where the silent and
mysterious Cliff Forrester has been living in seclusion
for years....

WATCH FOR ALL TWELVE BOOKS OF THE TYLER SERIES
Available wherever Harlequin books are sold

TYLER-G

Back by Popular Demand

Janet Dailey

Americana

A romantic tour of America through fifty favorite
Harlequin Presents, each set in a different state
researched by Janet and her husband, Bill. A journey
of a lifetime in one cherished collection.

In January, don't miss the exciting states featured in:

Available wherever
Harlequin books are sold.

Rebels & Rogues

All men are not created equal. Some are rough around the edges. Tough-minded but tenderhearted. Incredibly sexy. The tempting fulfillment of every woman's fantasy.

When it's time to fight for what they believe in, to win that special woman, our Rebels and Rogues are heroes at heart.

Josh: He swore never to play the hero . . . unless the price was right.

THE PRIVATE EYE by Jayne Ann Krentz.
Temptation #377, January 1992.

Matt: A hard man to forget . . . and an even harder man not to love.

THE HOOD by Carin Rafferty.
Temptation #381, February 1992.

At Temptation, 1992 is the Year of Rebels and Rogues. Look for twelve exciting stories about bold and courageous men, one each month. Don't miss upcoming books from your favorite authors, including Candace Schuler, JoAnn Ross and Janice Kaiser.

Available wherever Harlequin books are sold.   RR-1

***Harlequin Superromance*®**
Family ties...

SEVENTH HEAVEN
In the introduction to the Osborne family trilogy,
Kate Osborne finds her destiny with Police
Commissioner Donovan Cade.

Available in December

ON CLOUD NINE
Kate's second daughter, Juliet, has old-fashioned
values like her mother's. But those values are tested
when she meets Ross Stafford, a jazz musician,
sometime actor and teaching assistant . . . and the
object of her younger sister's affections. Can Juliet
only achieve her heart's desire at the cost of her
integrity?

Coming in January

SWINGING ON A STAR
Meridee is Kate's oldest daughter, but very much her
own person. Determined to climb the corporate
ladder, she has never had time for love. But her life is
turned upside down when Zeb Farrell storms into
town determined to eliminate jobs in her company—
her sister's among them! Meridee is prepared to do
battle, but for once she's met her match.

Coming in February

H A R L E Q U I N

A Calendar of Romance

Be a part of American Romance's year-long celebration of love and the holidays of 1992. Experience all the passion of falling in love during the excitement of each month's holiday. Some of your favorite authors will help you celebrate those special times of the year, like the revelry of New Year's Eve, the romance of Valentine's Day, the magic of St. Patrick's Day.

Start counting down to the new year with

#421 HAPPY NEW YEAR, DARLING
by Margaret St. George

Read all the books in *A Calendar of Romance*, coming to you one each month, all year, from Harlequin American Romance.

American Romance®

COR1